POLITICS AND WHISKEY
DON'T MIX

Raider lifted his glass. "To the great state of Wyomin'."

There was a cheer.

Then somebody was laughing.

Raider looked across the room to see a rough man sitting by himself at a table. He was stocky and wore a gray slicker and a pointed Stetson. He hadn't shaved for a while. He had a hateful laugh.

"Somethin' funny?" Raider asked him.

One of the barflies gaped at Raider. "That's Harley Dixon, stranger. Don't cross him. We ain't got no law in..."

Raider waved the man off. "I want to hear what Mr. Harley Dixon wants to say. Go on, Harley."

The man frowned at him. "This godforsaken terr'tory ain't never gonna be a state. Too many idiots around here. Like you." He pointed right at Raider.

Raider squared his shoulders, still smiling at the man. "Ain't no need to be mean about it."

Dixon started to stand up.

Raider dropped his hand beside his Peacemaker.

Dixon froze in the wooden chair.

The bar crowd scattered in a hurry.

Raider watched the man's hands. "It's a bad day for dyin', Harley."

Other books in the RAIDER series by
J. D. HARDIN

RAIDER
SIXGUN CIRCUS
THE YUMA ROUNDUP
THE GUNS OF EL DORADO
THIRST FOR VENGEANCE
DEATH'S DEAL
VENGEANCE RIDE
CHEYENNE FRAUD
THE GULF PIRATES
TIMBER WAR
SILVER CITY AMBUSH
THE NORTHWEST RAILROAD WAR
THE MADMAN'S BLADE
WOLF CREEK FEUD
BAJA DIABLO
STAGECOACH RANSOM
RIVERBOAT GOLD
WILDERNESS MANHUNT
SINS OF THE GUNSLINGER
BLACK HILLS TRACKDOWN
GUNFIGHTER'S SHOWDOWN
THE ANDERSON VALLEY SHOOT-OUT
BADLANDS PATROL
THE YELLOWSTONE THIEVES
THE ARKANSAS HELLRIDER
BORDER WAR
THE EAST TEXAS DECEPTION
DEADLY AVENGERS
HIGHWAY OF DEATH
THE PINKERTON KILLERS
TOMBSTONE TERRITORY
MEXICAN SHOWDOWN
THE CALIFORNIA KID
BORDER LAW
HANGMAN'S LAW
FAST DEATH
DESERT DEATH TRAP

RAIDER

WYOMING AMBUSH

J.D. HARDIN

BERKLEY BOOKS, NEW YORK

WYOMING AMBUSH

A Berkley Book/published by arrangement with
the author

PRINTING HISTORY
Berkley edition/August 1990

All rights reserved.
Copyright © 1990 by The Berkley Publishing Group.
This book may not be reproduced in whole or in part,
by mimeograph or any other means, without permission.
For information address: The Berkley Publishing Group,
200 Madison Avenue, New York, New York 10016.

ISBN: 0-425-12222-0

A BERKLEY BOOK® TM 757,375
Berkley Books are published by The Berkley Publishing Group,
200 Madison Aveunue, New York, New York 10016.
The name "BERKLEY" and the "B" logo
are trademarks belonging to the Berkley Publishing Corporation.

PRINTED IN THE UNITED STATES OF AMERICA

10 9 8 7 6 5 4 3 2 1

**This book is dedicated to
Charlie "Butch" Parsons**

CHAPTER ONE

Raider pulled back on the reins of the big sorrel mare, skidding to a stop on the dusty Colorado plain. At least he thought it was the Colorado plain. He had come a long way from Kansas, heading northwest through the top corner of Colorado, chasing an outlaw named Rattler Rogers. Rogers had killed and robbed with a wide-sweeping hand that covered most of the north-central plain. And Raider still hadn't been able to find him after a month of searching.

He urged the mare into a walk. She was a strong animal, never seeming to tire. Raider took the time to rest her at night. She didn't like the darkness very much. Too skittish to ride after sundown, so that limited his chasing hours from dawn till dusk.

The tall Pinkerton agent, the rough-hewn native of Arkansas, took a deep breath of the cool air that surrounded him. It was late September, which meant that it could snow almost anytime once you got into the Rockies. He strained his black eyes, peering toward the horizon, wondering if the vague impressions were the highest peaks of the mountains or just clouds gathered against a distant sky.

Where the hell was he, anyway? Raider never used maps much, relying on the stars and the sun to guide him. He had been able to find Sterling, a small town near where Colorado, Nebraska, and Wyoming came together. A man matching the description of Rattler Rogers had robbed the general store there, killing the proprietor and his squaw wife and mortally wounding the only lawman, a marshal out of Denver.

Raider shifted in the saddle, feeling the pains of a long day's ride. What if Rattler had turned west-southwest, toward Denver? No, the snake would keep going, away from the big towns. He would probably bypass Cheyenne and Laramie if he went into Wyoming. He could always go east, over into Nebraska. Hell, once he got into north country there were a hundred places he could hole up.

The sorrel snorted as the sun disappeared. Raider could see the high peaks of the mountains against the reddish sky. Soon the rolling plain and foothills would change into rocky passes and snowcaps. No, those were clouds. The mare snorted again.

Raider patted the animal's neck. "Okay, scaredy cat, I'll stop in a few minutes. I want to see if there's water hereabouts."

He spurred her into a run, hoping she wouldn't notice the lengthening of the shadows.

He reached the small river while there was still a little light left. He managed to gather enough dried brush and groundwood to build a campfire. The sorrel was content to stay tied by the glow of the flames. Raider took off the saddle and made himself a bedroll.

So far, the nights had been good to him. Not warm, but not icy either. He slept pretty good by the fire, and his bones didn't ache when he woke up. He hoped it stayed that way until he found Rattler.

He had been dreaming about snakes lately, but he always managed to shoot them in his dreams. They could strike quick, but he was quicker.

He settled in next to the fire.

His saddlebags were beside him. He reached into the pocket for a can of beans that he had purchased from the new general store owner in Sterling. The hunting knife from his boot served as a can opener and a spoon. Raider didn't really notice the taste of the beans, he just wanted to fill his belly so he could keep going for another day.

The sorrel lifted her head and sniffed the wind.

Raider reached for his '76 Winchester, pulling the rifle from its scabbard. He stood up, listening. Anybody who met him on the trail would have thought he was a bandit. He wore dusty blue jeans that looked gray, a faded but thick cotton shirt, leather vest, crusty boots that would be shined as soon as he caught the outlaw, and a black Stetson that needed to be cleaned and blocked. A heavy shearling coat protected him from the chilly fog of morning, but for now he used it as a pillow.

When the mare lowered her head, Raider sat down again. He reached for the holster that hung coiled on the horn of his saddle. The Colt .45 Peacemaker felt good in his hand. He spun the cylinder to make sure it was working right, then aimed and pulled the trigger. There was a click on the empty chamber.

Raider repeated the motion, frowning at the second click of the hammer. Something was wrong. He dry-fired a third time. He felt the give in the spring. It was weakening inside the pistol. Best to get it to a gunsmith as soon as possible. If the spring went, it might mean the difference between catching his quarry or dying in the process.

He slipped the Peacemaker back into the holster, worrying the way a parent worries over a child. He wouldn't feel right until the spring was replaced in the Peacemaker. Best to keep his rifle handy at all times.

He leaned back against the saddle, peering into the flames of the fire. The big man was becoming sadly aware that he hadn't gained much ground on Rattler Rogers. If he counted the robbery in Sterling, Rogers had almost a week's head start. A whole damned week.

He cast a glance at the sorrel. He should have traded her in Sterling for a horse that would run at night. That was always his edge on an outlaw. Ride at night, sleep in the saddle, stop only for a couple of hours to rest his mount and eat something.

He looked at the fire again. The flames were hypnotic. He tried to consider his alternatives. He could turn toward Denver, find a new horse, and see if Rattler had been in town, but all his instincts told him to push on north. Maybe he'd find a rancher with a mount to sell. Any trader of horses would jump at the chance to buy the sorrel, she was so damned tall and strong. Nobody else would be bothered by the fact that she didn't like to run at night.

She snorted again.

Raider stood up, holding the rifle.

He was far enough north to happen on a pack of wolves. Bears usually didn't venture down onto the plain, but wolves did. Coyotes were scared, but wolves would come in and attack a horse if they were hungry enough.

Raider threw some more wood on the fire. Even if the wolves didn't come to attack, they might still come to drink from the river. What the hell river was it, anyway? Maybe the Lodgepole. That would mean he had crossed over into Wyoming.

The mare settled down finally, and Raider got into his bedroll again, but he couldn't sleep. His head had gone to work, considering what else might spook a horse. There were still a few renegade Indians around—a few Sioux braves who didn't like being crammed into a reservation. Several Shoshone renegades had gained reputations as well.

He considered putting out the fire but decided it didn't matter—if an Indian had seen the flames, he would already know where Raider was. He wouldn't be able to hide from a Sioux or a Shoshone in the dark. And the fire would discourage wolves, if they were out there on the black plain.

Raider kept the Winchester resting over his legs, ready for anything or anyone. He went back to thinking about Rattler Rogers. He'd have to pick up a trail soon, or it might mean a defeat for him—the first time he had been sent out to find a man and couldn't come back with the prisoner in custody.

He had always dreaded his first failure, which was probably what kept him working so hard all the time.

He laughed to himself. What would Pinkerton and Wagner say about the man who got away from Raider? Would they use his failure as an excuse to fire him? Raider knew the agency wasn't wild about his strong-arm methods: using a fist and a gun to bring outlaws to justice. Yet they always sent him new cases, new fish to fry, new mysteries to solve.

Only, Rattler Rogers wasn't much of a mystery. Just an outlaw who was running north. Just a man with a price on his head. Just...

The mare raised her front hooves off the ground, whinnying, stomping the dirt. Raider came up again with the rifle. His head turned as he peered into the darkness. He couldn't hear a thing.

The sorrel kept kicking the ground.

Raider levered the Winchester, jacking a cartridge into the chamber.

He suddenly wished he hadn't camped with his back to the river.

The mare tried to pull away from the bush where she was tied.

Raider reached for her reins.

A horrible cry welled from the mare's throat.

Raider then heard the low growling as the wolf rushed out of the darkness. He wheeled to his right, swinging the Winchester. But it was too late.

The wolf made a spectacular leap, sailing through the air, landing on the sorrel's neck.

Raider started to fire the Winchester, but he was suddenly aware of the rest of the pack rushing in on him.

As the Winchester erupted, Raider had a terrible feeling that he would never be able to kill them all.

CHAPTER TWO

William Wagner strode briskly down Fifth Avenue, heading away from the Pinkerton National Detective Agency, making a beeline for the Western Union office. It was late evening in Chicago, but the streets were still alive with citizens enjoying a pleasant Indian summer. Wagner hoped the key operator at the telegraph office had not forgotten his promise to stay open a few extra hours. Wagner had sent over an envelope full of money to make sure the man stuck to his duty.

Much to Wagner's chagrin, the door to the Western Union office was locked. He banged on the door, bruising his knuckles in a fit of anger. Passersby on the dark street steered around him, no doubt thinking he was a deranged individual.

A lamplight swelled inside the office.

Wagner strained to peer through the smoky window.

Somebody moved toward the door. "Who's there?"

"It's me, Wagner. Have you forgotten?"

He saw the man put a hand to his forehead. "I knew there was a reason I stayed here so late."

"Open the door!"

The key operator ushered Wagner into the office.

Wagner glared at the man, who didn't seem to notice.

"Sorry, Mr. Wagner. I reckon I had just about given up on you. It's almost nine o'clock."

"I seem to recall an envelope that was delivered here by messenger today," Wagner offered.

"And it's appreciated too, sir."

The key operator started behind the counter. He never paid much attention to Wagner. The dapper man from the Pinkerton Agency was always acting sort of snotty, but the operator knew that he really didn't mean anything by it.

Wagner removed his wire-rimmed spectacles and started to clean the lenses, a nervous habit that he repeated endlessly throughout his day. "I know this is difficult on you," Wagner said in a kinder tone, "but Mr. Pinkerton is going out of town for a while, and there are many matters that he needs to attend to before he leaves."

"Oh? Where's he goin'?"

"I'm afraid that's confidential," Wagner replied.

The man shrugged. "You was the one who brought it up."

Wagner blushed a little, as if he could not bear to be confronted with his own snobbery. "Yes, I'm sorry, I suppose I did."

Reaching for his desk, the key operator grabbed a bundle of messages that had been tied together with string. "Reckon it's the busy time of the year," he said. "Key's been tappin' all day."

Wagner quickly untied the string and began to leaf through the messages. Several cases had been solved, and few were still pending. Pinkerton would just have to live with the news. There was no way to have everything wrapped up tidily before he left town.

"Anythin' goin' out?" The operator was looking at him, his pencil ready to write. "I mean, I can't send it until tomorrow . . ."

Wagner nodded. "Let me think for a moment."

He lifted one of the messages, wondering what Pinkerton would do.

Finally he said, "Tell Stokes to sit tight until he gets further word from the agency."

"That'd be goin' to Missouri?"

Wagner nodded. "Yes, put it on our account."

"All right, sir."

Wagner frowned. "Nothing came in from Raider? Nothing from Kansas, or maybe Nebraska?"

The operator gestured to the bundle of messages. "If it ain't in there, I ain't received it."

Wagner thought the man was terribly common in his speech and mannerisms. He felt superior to him, at least until the telegraph key began to click behind them. The operator lifted his ear and listened.

"Maybe that's from Raider," Wagner offered.

The man was silent until the key stopped. "No, that was just the line operator askin' for a test. Hmm. Wonder what he's doin' out this late?"

Wagner frowned at the man. "You mean you could decipher that code simply by listening to it."

The man smiled at him. "Mr. Wagner, we're all good at somethin'. I'm good at this. You're good at . . . well, whatever you're good at."

Wagner ignored him, leafing through the messages again. He was worried because he hadn't heard from Raider in a month. Everybody else seemed to be checking in at regular intervals. Not Raider, though.

"Everything okay, Mr. Wagner?"

He smiled, realizing that he liked the key operator a great deal. The man was reliable, if somewhat slow in his manner. The agency relied on him for a lot of important messages, telegrams from all over the country.

"Thank you for staying open," he told the man.

"You're welcome, sir."

"By the way, what's your name?"

"Aw, you'll just forget it, Mr. Wagner. You ask my name ever' time you come here and then you forget it before you're halfway back to the office."

Wagner stiffened. "Well, if that's how you feel about it!"

He turned and left the office, carrying his bundle of papers.

The key operator had to laugh as he closed the door and turned the key in the lock. He knew Wagner had the disposition of a persnickity, educated man. He wouldn't hold it against him. Wagner was just worried about his men, especially the one called Raider.

The operator decided to stay an extra hour, just in case a wire came in from the agent who caused William Wagner so much consternation.

CHAPTER THREE

When Raider fired the Winchester, the leader of the wolf pack fell into the dirt, yelping and turning circles on the ground, dying.

Suddenly the rest of them were gone, dispersed into the shadows.

Raider wheeled and fired from the hip, shooting the animal that clung to the neck of the sorrel mare.

The wolf fell into the dust, dead. Raider had hit him squarely in the head. He started to check the horse's neck, but growling came from his left. Another charge.

He saw the shape against the fire, the animal leaping at him, bared fangs and cold eyes.

Raider swung the rifle, catching the wolf's snout with the butt of the weapon. The animal hit the ground. Raider fired the Winchester and killed it before it could move again.

Another charge from the darkness.

He spun, levering the Winchester, shooting from the hip.

Two more wolves fell into the dirt.

How many were there in all?

Shapes of canine forms circled just outside the light of the fire.

They must've really wanted the sorrel to stay on it like this. Raider considered letting them have the animal, but he finally decided that he wasn't the sort of man to surrender, not when he could still fight.

The mare whinnied sorrowful-like.

Raider stepped closer to the animal, checking the marks on its neck. The wolf had bitten deep. Blood ran down the poor mare's hide. Raider would have to get a poultice on the wound before it festered. A damned bite was the worst. He'd be shit out of luck if the sorrel died on him.

"Easy, pardner."

Something moved toward the fire.

Raider shot at the shape but missed.

They were out there, but they were biding their time.

He had to do something about the animal's neck. If he could get to the river, maybe he could find some clay. Pack it tight with some straw. But he'd have to take the animal with him, and that meant leaving the fire.

Better reload before he did anything.

He knelt down next to his saddlebags, reaching for a couple of the rifle cartridges. The wolves must've known something. Two of them rushed from the darkness. Raider levered the rifle, firing twice, catching one of the animals and scaring the other one off.

The sorrel snorted behind him.

A doglike form seemed to be nipping at its hindquarters.

Raider pulled the trigger of the Winchester only to hear a harmless click. He reached for the Colt on the saddle horn. One round dispatched the hateful creature to hell. He slipped the .45 in his belt.

"How many of you bastards am I gonna have to kill!" he cried.

They smelled the damned blood. They weren't going to leave until they had their dinner. Maybe he should just give them the mare.

No. A Pinkerton never quit. Just reload. Get the cartridges in the rifle. Blast the hell out of all of them.

Two more came in behind him.

Raider wheeled, using the Colt, streaming gunfire that scared the two wolves back into the shadows.

He slid more cartridges into the side load of the Winchester. When the rifle was full, he went back to the sorrel.

The blood still flowed from the mare's neck. He had to stop it or he'd be stuck on the plain without a mount. He needed to get her down to the riverbank. And the best way to do that was to ride her.

Raider swung onto the bare back of the mare. He seized the reins and turned her toward the water. She bolted, running frantically away from the dog-demons that waited in the darkness.

The wolves followed, excited by the flight of their prey and the smell of thick blood.

It wasn't far to the water. The mare stopped by the river, raising up, lifting her hooves. Raider felt himself sliding off her back. He hit the sandy bank with a thud.

The mare bolted away from him, heading back toward the fire.

Raider heard the growls when the wolves got her. The mare let out a tortured cry. Raider cocked the rifle and fired in the direction of the hellish rumble.

The wolves backed off again.

Raider ran until he found the sorrel. She was lying on her side, her throat torn out. They had really wanted her.

He fired a shot to put her out of her misery.

The dark shapes came at him again.

Raider lifted the rifle to fire. A harmless click resounded instead of a bullet. Empty again. He pulled the Colt from his belt, thumbing back the hammer, squeezing the trigger.

One shot chased them to the side.

He could hear them yelping and nipping at one another.

He took aim with the Colt, hoping to chase them even further. But when he pulled the trigger, the hammer of the weapon did not fall. He felt the spring go inside. The .45 was useless.

Low growls seemed to form a circle around him.

He grabbed the rifle, holding the barrel like a club. "Come on, you bastards!"

He started slowly toward the fire, which still burned near his saddle. Get back to reload. Then he'd show them something.

WYOMING AMBUSH   13

Another charge. A wolf leaped, coming straight for him. Raider swung the rifle and clipped the wolf. A yelp. The animal scurried away.

Raider wondered if they would leave him alone when he was far enough away from the corpse of the sorrel. He hated giving up the poor mare. But she wouldn't have lived long anyway, not with that chunk out of her throat.

He made it back to the fire in a few minutes. Kneeling by his saddlebag again, he began to reload. They wouldn't bother him now. Not if . . .

Two of them rushed out of the darkness. They both leapt at the same time, coming from different directions. Raider lifted the rifle, cranking the lever. But then the damned thing jammed on him and it was too late.

Both animals hit him at the same time. He reached for them, trying to grab a hunk of fur, a throat, a muzzle. They all rolled together. Then he felt teeth and claws.

This was it.

The end.

Killed by two wolves.

Then there were two loud bursts of gunfire and the dogs weren't bothering him anymore.

The wolves startled when they heard the blast from the scattergun.

They got off him, but the shotgun erupted again and both of them fell dead next to Raider.

He lay still, wondering if he was hurt as bad as the sorrel. He felt scratches and sore spots. But there didn't seem to be any great gushing of his precious blood.

More gunfire lit up the night.

Somebody was shooting down by the river, where the sorrel had fallen.

Raider got up and started to search for his Winchester in the dark. He had to feel bad about both of his guns malfunctioning on him. Sometimes luck just didn't swing your way.

He found the rifle and turned toward the river.

Where the hell was the man who had saved him from the wolves?

More shots by the sorrel.

Somebody was finishing off the pack.

Raider moved slowly toward the source of the shooting. Had to be Indians. Who else could hunt in the dark?

The fire had been extinguished. Had a Sioux brave kicked it out? Or had it finally died on its own?

Raider kept moving until he tripped over something. He went headlong across the body of the mare, falling into the sand. There was a dead wolf lying right next to him.

He started to get up.

Then he heard the clicking of two hammers.

Probably a double-barreled scattergun, he thought, the same one that had killed the wolves.

"Don't move, sir." The voice was deep and ominous. "Stay right there."

It belonged to a white man.

Raider held his breath, watching as the shape finally came into view. A big man stood over him. And the man was holding the scattergun with both barrels pointed right at the wide-eyed Pinkerton.

Raider figured that the friendly approach was best when a stranger had the drop on him. "Looks like this was somethin' of a big mess," he said to the shadowy figure. "Them dogs liked to kilt me."

Nothing from the man with the scattergun.

"You hear me, pardner?"

"I hear you."

Raider started to get up.

The cold iron of the scattergun pressed against his neck. "I told you to stay still, sir."

He eased back down. "I'm stayin' still, pardner."

The man with the shotgun took a deep breath. "Well, I think I got 'em all."

"Yeah, I reckon..."

Pressure from the scattergun. "You don't talk yet," the stranger said. "Not about them wolves anyways."

"Just let me know what you want to hear, pardner." At least until I can get the drop on you, Raider thought to himself. Then we'll see who talks about what.

"What are you doin' on my land?" the shotgun man asked.

"Your land? I thought I was on the prairie. I thought this was Colorado."

"This is Wyoming," the man replied. "And you're on the Double-W Ranch. You're twenty miles south of Rock River."

Raider suddenly forgot about the shotgun on his neck. "Rock River? Damn, I really am lost. I thought I was headin' for Cheyenne. I musta gone around it. Damn, I'll never catch Rogers now."

The barrel lifted from his neck. "Rogers?"

Raider figured it was best to be truthful, especially if he was trespassing on the land of an honest rancher. "I'm a Pinkerton agent, sir. Chasin' a man name of Rattler Rogers. Last I heard, he was headin' this way."

"Pinkerton, huh?"

"That's right."

A pause. Then: "You need a hand, Pinkerton?"

"I could use one, pardner."

The stranger helped Raider to his feet. "I'm William Walters," he said. "My friends call me Big Bill."

He offered his hand.

Raider shook with him. "I reckon I don't have to be afraid of that scattergun anymore."

"Not unless you cross me," Walters replied. "Come on. Let's build a fire and see if we can clean up this mess."

Raider helped the stranger gather brush and groundwood. It didn't take them long to rekindle the embers of the campfire that had gone out. When the flames swelled, Raider got a better look at the man with the scattergun.

William Walters fit his nickname. He was a big, round, rough-looking man with a thick mustache. He wore a pointed Stetson with a round brim, the kind of hat favored by men in the north. He also wore a long coat made from some sort of fur, maybe a bear skin. An older man, but still strong and healthy.

Raider watched as Big Bill fashioned two torches from brush. "I hate to ask you," he said to the big man, "but I was wonderin' if you'd help me find all those dead critters. I want the skins."

Raider nodded. "You saved my hide, so I reckon I owe

you. Where'd you come from? And what're you doin' out here by yourself?"

Walters pointed west. "My lodge is about ten miles that way. I got cattle all over this range. Those dogs been givin' us trouble, among other things."

"What other things?"

Walters waved him off. "My trouble ain't none of your'n, mister. If you'd just help me get these animals in a pile, I'll be thankful."

Raider said he would be happy to help.

Walters lit two torches and handed one of them to Raider. It took a while to find the carcasses—twelve in all, looking harmless stacked next to the fire. Raider shook his head in wonder.

"What?" Walters asked.

"They wanted that horse pretty bad," the big man replied. "I couldn't scare 'em off with my Winchester."

Walters pointed west. "Cattle brings 'em here from the high country. It's easier to bring down a steer. Cows don't run as fast as mule deer and elk."

Raider eyed the burly rancher. "You got courage to go a-huntin' on your own, Walters."

A shrug from Big Bill. "One of my men is roamin' hereabouts. Though I can't say he'll even come runnin' when he hears all the shootin'. Hell, I ain't got a shootist or a frontiersman amongst 'em."

"You seem somethin' of a mountain man," Raider offered.

Walters laughed. "No, I can't say as I am. Shouldn't be talkin' like that. It's just... well, I was born and raised in Wyomin'. Mighta been the first white man borned here for all I know. Went back east durin' the war to make my fortune on the railroads. But I come back now. Used a lot of my money to buy land hereabouts. Now I got the Double-W. You know, for my name. Yes, sir, I come a long way."

Raider suddenly frowned and looked into the fire. "A long way. That's how far I come. Now that my mount is dead, I'll never catch Rogers."

"Yes you will," Walters offered.

Raider looked up at the burly rancher. "Come again?"

"Man named Rattler Rogers has been causin' trouble up

near Elk Mountain. Been stealin' from the locals. Hell, I think he stole from me when he came through here. Leastways, I found a steer that had been shot to death. Some of it had been taken away. That was just what I needed, what with these wolves and ever'thing else that's been goin' on."

Raider stood up. "Elk Mountain? Where the hell is it?"

"West and a little north," Walters replied.

"How long has Rattler been at it?"

"Well, it usually takes me a couple of days to get the gossip from Elk Mountain, so I'd say he's been there at least a week."

Raider clapped his hands together. "How far is it?"

"Not even a day's ride. They say Rogers is hidin' in the forest. There ain't no law up that way. Not yet. Just a few miners, some loners, a couple of families diggin' for silver and tryin' to farm."

Raider exhaled. "That's the perfect place for him to hole up. Damn. I wish them dogs had stayed away from my horse."

Walters gestured toward his own mount, a tall black stallion. "Take my animal, Pinkerton."

Raider gawked at the man. "You mean it?"

"Can I trust you to bring it back?"

Raider nodded. "If it lives. Other than that, I can only promise to come back and pay you for it."

Walters waved to the west. "Go on. Get him. You'll be doin' all of us a favor. We don't need that kind in Wyoming."

Raider felt the sweat breaking over his forehead. He quickly found his gear, including the jammed Winchester. It only took him a few minutes to get it working again. His Colt may have been useless, but the rifle would be enough to bring down Rattler Rogers.

He jumped into the saddle of the stallion, peering down at Big Bill. "What're you gonna ride, Walters?"

The rancher shrugged. "My man'll be along direckly. And I'll keep your saddle for collateral."

Raider wasn't sure what collateral was, but he didn't have time to wait.

Walters threw the big man his saddlebags. "Hope to see you again, Pinkerton."

"Name's Raider."

"Good luck, Raider."

He turned the stallion west, thanking the Good Lord for men like Big Bill. At first, he wondered if the black liked to run in the dark. But the animal held steady, charging headlong through the night as if it feared nothing on the rolling plain.

CHAPTER FOUR

The stallion was a great horse. It had everything that a mount needed—speed, strength, courage, stamina. It carried Raider toward Elk Mountain, staying steady, never seeming to breathe hard. Walters had been a hell of a trusting man to loan him the animal. He hadn't even asked to see Raider's Pinkerton credentials.

As he rode on through the dark, Raider began to wonder if maybe Big Bill had been trying to get rid of him. Gave him the horse because he was up to no good and he wanted the Pinkerton out of the way.

What difference did it make? Raider had a mount and he was on the trail of Rattler Rogers. Unless Big Bill had been lying to him. He had been awfully quick to trust the rancher—if he was a rancher.

Raider shook it off. If Walters had pointed him in the wrong direction, he could surely double back later and give him hell for it. Until then, he had to follow the only lead that presented itself.

By dawn, he was well into the foothills. A large peak seemed to rise above the others. Elk Mountain? He rode up on a crude sign that pointed west, saying: "Pass to Elk Mountain. Try it if you mean it."

Raider meant it.

He guided the stallion along a narrow path until he came to a trickle of water. Dismounting, he let the animal drink from the rill. He bent to wet his own lips and cleanse the minor wounds from his tangle with the wolf pack.

When the stallion had drunk enough, he began to walk, pulling the animal behind him. The path was rocky, unfit for riding. Raider wondered how long he would have to stay on foot.

Trees began to rise above the path, prompting Raider to take his rifle from the scabbard on Walters's saddle.

Too many shadows between the tree trunks.

Good place for an ambush.

Raider stayed close to his mount, hoping that a stray bushwhacker's bullet didn't kill the borrowed horse. He hated riding an animal that didn't belong to him. Still, he'd rather lose the stallion than his own life.

The trail widened a little.

Raider came out onto a ledge that looked down into a valley. He could see the settlement of Elk Mountain below him. It looked dark and tiny in the distance. Not much of a town.

He had to go back into the trees for a while, taking the path as it began to slope downward. The day warmed, bringing the forest to life. Birds flitted among the green branches. making more noise than a whole war party of stalking Comanches.

The sounds of the forest didn't seem to bother the stallion. Raider kept a close watch on him, figuring he would spook at the sign of real trouble. He also scanned the trees, searching for movement that might belong to a gunman.

Walters had said that Rattler Rogers was operating *near* Elk Mountain. If that was true, the outlaw could have been anywhere in the trees, waiting for a victim.

Raider stayed on the shady side of the stallion, continuing down the path. He realized it was going to be a long trek to the slapdash community that lay on the other side of the valley. He could always stop and rest for a while, but hell, he didn't feel tired. If anything, he was raring to go. Get Rattler Rogers in his sights. Squeeze the trigger slowly.

Of course, he would have to give Rogers a chance to surrender peaceably. No sense killing him if it wasn't necessary. Take him back to stand trial. See him hang from the fat end of a noose.

The path flattened out at the bottom of the slope. The forest still surrounded him, but at least he could ride now if he had to. He kept close to the stallion, walking, ready to mount up.

He went on until he heard the shooting.

When the echo reached the big man, he stopped, listening, wondering how far he was from the gunman.

Maybe it was just somebody hunting.

Another shot.

It sounded like a rifle.

More return fire, softer echoes, like pistols.

The rifle had the last word, and then the shooting stopped.

Raider swung into the saddle, crooking the Winchester in his left arm and holding the reins with his right hand.

The stallion was ready to run. It bolted forward at Raider's slight urging. The big Pinkerton barreled down the narrow trail, wondering if he was even close to the source of the commotion.

It took him almost an hour to find the bodies. Three of them. Face-down in a flowing stream.

He dismounted, splashing through the water that barely rose over the tops of his boots. Two men and a girl. Raider saw the pistol in the girl's cold hand. Somebody had shot the men, and the girl had come out shooting. Come out from where?

Raider glanced up to see the crude cabin that lay back in the trees. She had come from there, wielding the pistol, then the ambusher had shot her, too. What the hell had he been after?

Surely the two men hadn't been panning for gold. Not here in Wyoming. Maybe they were coming from their silver dig. Raider figured he would find a hole in the mountain if he looked hard enough.

He pulled the bodies out of the stream, laying them beside each other in a grotesque row.

The girl didn't look much older than twelve or thirteen. The men were probably her father and brother. Where the hell had they come from, looking for a mother lode?

Clues would be found in the cabin.

He would have a look-see.

Anything to keep from burying the bodies right away. He would have to do it, though. He owed the dead ones that much.

He grabbed the reins of the black, taking the rifle from Walters's scabbard. His approach to the cabin was slow. What if the ambusher was still there? Hell, it had to be Rattler who was causing all the trouble.

The cabin was empty. Raider rummaged around until he had enough information. They were from Indiana. Had been registering silver at the assay office for almost a year. The ambusher had torn the cabin apart to look for the dead family's life savings. Raider wondered if he had found it.

He left the cabin, thinking that he should ride to Elk Mountain to raise a posse. Get some of the locals to help him. Corner the rattler like a snake in a cotton bin.

But he never got to mount the stallion. A rifle exploded, kicking up the ground next to his feet. The black spooked, rearing. Raider dived back toward the cabin to escape the slugs that seemed to follow him as he rolled.

He managed to get indoors.

The rifle chattered, splintering the wood of the cabin's outside wall.

He heard the black as it ran away from him.

More rifle fire.

Had the stallion been hit?

The rifle was quiet all of a sudden.

Raider realized he was holding his own Winchester. Draw fire and take a bead. Return the favor.

He took off his hat and placed it on the barrel of his rifle. Then he got low, peeking around the edge of the open doorway. Lifting the hat above him, he coaxed the enemy rifle into giving away its position. His Stetson flew off the end of his Winchester, but it didn't matter. He had the gunman marked.

Raider aimed and fired the '76 several times. That shut him up. For a while anyway. A few minutes later the rifle returned fire from another location. Raider had to mark him all over again.

But he didn't shoot this time. Instead he stayed low, crawling toward a window in the back of the cabin. No sense wasting all his bullets—not while he could sneak out and stalk the bushwhacker. Stalk him like the animal that he was. Take him. Dead or alive. It no longer mattered to the big man.

Raider rolled through the window and dropped to the ground below.

He looked up a steep slope that rose into the woods. Maybe he should climb. Circle around. The bushwhacker was on the other side of the creek, hiding in a cottonwood thicket.

Raider peeked around the side of the cabin, trying to get a view of the creek. Trees were in his way. What the hell was he going to do?

He had become the hunter, so he had to think that way. And any good hunter knew that you had to let the game come to you. Stalk it for a while, mark its trail, and then take a hiding place to wait.

Raider flinched when the enemy rifle kicked up again.

The slugs slammed around the doorway.

Quiet again.

Raider held steady. If he didn't return fire, maybe the bushwhacker would think he was dead. It had to be Rogers. The rattler striking from under a dark rock.

Gazing upward, he saw that the eave of the roof was close to the incline at the far side of the cabin. Raider crawled over and studied the angle. It wouldn't be hard to get up there. Just use some of the saplings for a handhold. He could see why the dead miner had built his cabin at the base of the slope—it was protected from the rear by the mountain.

Too bad that the family hadn't been protected in the middle of the stream.

Raider figured to get even for all three of them.

He climbed up the slope and rolled onto the roof. Hesitating, he felt the roof beneath him. It gave a little. Would it be strong enough to support his weight?

He started to crawl toward the apex of the roof. The dead man had done a good job. The rafters held him fine. He peeked over the edge of the crest, looking toward the creek.

The sun was high now, and everything was bathed in rich light.

He listened in the stillness of midday. Even the birds were

quiet now, except for a covey of partridges that suddenly shot out of the trees.

Somebody moved in the boughs of evergreens.

Raider took aim, but finally decided that the man was out of range. And he really couldn't see him anyway. A juniper bush would deflect a rifle slug as well as a brick wall.

Wait—that's what he'd have to do. A good hunter always had patience, and Raider was a good hunter.

The man came out of the trees and splashed clumsily into the stream.

Raider kept a bead on him.

His thumb clicked back the hammer of the Winchester.

Closer, you bastard.

The man splashed across the stream. He was carrying a Winchester, and he wore a sidearm. Raider couldn't tell for sure, but he figured the big handle had to indicate a Peacemaker or a Remington.

Raider had him in the sights of the '76.

The man stopped to look at the bodies that had been laid side by side on the bank of the stream.

Raider would have taken him if the tree branches hadn't been in his way. Even when the man started for the cabin, he stayed in the sight line of the thin forest. No way to hit him until he got right in front of the cabin.

But he was coming closer.

Patience. He remembered hunting with an old Arapaho Indian named Red Elk. They had waited all day for a big deer, but it had come.

Raider caught a glimpse of the man's hair. Dead blond, just like the poster said. The height and weight were right. It had to be the rattler.

He came into full view.

Raider wanted to take him. His finger tightened on the trigger. But he couldn't do it finally. Couldn't kill Rattler the way he had killed the mining family. He had to try to take him alive.

The big man squeezed the trigger of the rifle, hitting the dirt in front of Rattler Rogers.

The outlaw froze with his rifle in hand.

"Don't think it, Rogers," Raider called. "Not unless you want me to drop you where you stand."

Rogers still didn't move.

Raider put a round next to his toe. "Drop the rifle, Rogers, or the next one goes through your chest."

The outlaw quickly threw the gun on the ground in front of him.

"Now back away two steps," Raider went on. "Not three, not one. Two steps. That's right. Go on."

Rattler backed away from his rifle. "Who are you?" he called in a sick voice. "Who the hell are you?"

Raider kept him in the sight. If he turned to run, he would just have to shoot the rattler in the back. He told him so. Then he told him that he was a Pinkerton agent who had been sent to bring him back to Kansas.

Rattler smiled. "Pinkerton, huh? They had to send a Pinkerton to catch me. I'll be dogged."

"You're gonna be dead if you don't do what I say," Raider offered. "Now reach for your pistol with your left hand and drop it on the ground."

Rattler did as he was told, but Raider could still see the look in his shifty eyes. He knew the big man would have to come down off the roof. That would be the time to move.

Raider stood up, lowering the rifle to his hip. "Now I'm comin' down, Rattler. You just get spread-eagle on the ground. Go on."

The outlaw lay flat on his stomach with his arms and legs spread wide.

"That's good," Raider said. "Now, I'm gonna walk to the edge of the roof and jump down. I'll be fallin' for a second, but it won't be long enough for you to go for your gun. You got me?"

No reply.

"Answer me!"

"I got you."

"Good. Now stay real still while I . . ."

Raider had taken his first step forward. The plan had seemed right until that moment when the roof gave way underneath him. He fell into the cabin, pressed by the weight of the timbers that had fallen with him.

He could hear Rattler laughing outside the cabin.

He tried to move under the timbers.

Where was his rifle?

Rattler was moving toward him.

His damned head kept spinning, confusing him.

Damned roof, all moss and saplings.

His hands were still wrapped around the Winchester.

Rattler Rogers appeared at the door, watching the Pinkerton struggle.

He felt the hammer under his thumb.

The rifle was cocked.

Rattler Rogers lifted a Remington .44, pointing it straight at Raider's head. "Never killed a Pinkerton before."

Raider could see his figure in the doorway.

"You're gonna die, Pinkerton."

Rattler thumbed back the hammer of the .44.

He wanted to make Raider sweat.

The big man felt his finger on the trigger of the '76.

"It's gonna burn, Pinkerton. Burn bad and deep."

Raider could see the barrel of the Winchester from the corner of his eye. It was pointing straight at the door. Was the angle right?

Rattler made it better. He took a couple of steps toward the mess that lay on the floor of the cabin. Wanted a clearer shot. Wanted to torture the tall Pinkerton who had crashed through the roof.

Rattler's lips parted to say something.

Raider tripped the trigger of his rifle.

A long string of fire erupted from under the debris.

Rattler buckled. Blood poured from the left side of his body. He staggered backward, trying to aim the Remington. He fell before he was able to get off a shot.

Raider lay there for a minute, wondering if Rattler was really dead. A damned lucky shot. When the outlaw didn't move, Raider started to struggle, making his way out of the hateful rubble.

CHAPTER FIVE

Raider was ready to ride. It had taken him a long time to get there, but he was finally loaded up. He was glad to have it behind him.

When he had squirmed out from under the carnage, he had gone immediately to the stream and soaked his body in the cold water. Nothing broken. A few aches and pain. His pride hurt too.

Burying the bodies of the mining family had been the next task on his list. Plant them deep, so the animals wouldn't dig them up when they started to smell. Rock cairns to mark the graves. He'd have to get word to . . . to who? Who knew about this family with their little cabin in the valley?

But that was all behind him.

Finding the outlaw's horse had been the hardest part. Apparently the miners had not been in possession of a beast of burden, not even an old mule. So that had meant looking for the outlaw's horse, if he wanted to take the body with him.

And he had to take it. At least to a town where there was a wire. Then he could send word south to Kansas, to see if the authorities wanted proof that Rattler Rogers was dead. The horse had been tied in the cottonwoods.

So it was behind him. The hard part was over. A clear trail from here on. Raider wondered if he should ride into Elk Mountain. Let the locals see that the rattler wasn't going to bother them anymore.

He swung into the saddle of the stallion that had been loaned to him by William Walters. Rattler was lying crossways over the saddle of his own mount, a spindly looking roan. Raider wondered if the outlaw's horse would make it back to Kansas. He knew he should check the outlaw's saddlebags, but decided to let it wait.

Urging the black forward, he moved along the streambed, toward the path. He stopped, considering his options. The trail would lead him over the mountain, south. It would be a couple of days' ride to Cheyenne, maybe more. Elk Mountain was the other way, but it was a settlement. There might be food there, even whiskey. He didn't think that a place like Elk Mountain would provide any female companionship, but that didn't matter.

He was hungry, thirsty, tired.

Elk Mountain, it was.

He turned the black and started in the other direction.

The sun was sinking low, although there was still plenty of daylight left. Birds didn't bother him now. He was happy to hear them sing, to see them as they fluttered through the bushes.

After Elk Mountain, he would head south again. Probably have to go all the way to Cheyenne or Laramie to find a wire. He hoped like hell the Kansas authorities didn't want Rattler's body.

Why should they? As long as he was dead, what difference did it make? Their trouble was over.

And Rattler sure as hell didn't mind. He was sideways on his saddle, the dead man's ride.

Raider wondered if it would cause a ruckus when he finally rode into Elk Mountain.

"Confound it, Wagner, where's that..."

William Wagner thrust a sheaf of papers in front of his boss.

Allan Pinkerton snatched the papers from him. "I'm not going to be late for my train."

Wagner nodded. The office had been hell all morning. But they would be free soon. Pinkerton was taking an afternoon train to Kansas City. Then Wagner could settle down and get some work done.

Pinkerton turned toward his second-in-command, demanding facts from him. "Where's Stokes?"

"Still waiting," Wagner replied.

"Good. Send him to Iowa. That sounds like his sort of business."

Wagner nodded. He had already sent the telegram that morning. No need to let his boss know that he had been second-guessed.

"Avery?"

"He's coming in for a while," Wagner replied. "Wants to work closer to Chicago. I was thinking of putting him on bank duty."

Pinkerton said that would be fine. He pulled the pocket watch from his vest and grimaced. The time had come to depart. Pinkerton would never allow himself to be one minute late for anything.

"The carriage is waiting outside," Wagner said.

Pinkerton started for the door. "Where's my trunk?"

"On the coach." Wagner followed after him.

"Anderson," the big Scotsman said. "He wants to work in the field."

Pinkerton stopped at the entrance and turned for effect. "Well, William, do you think we should let Anderson work in the field?"

Wagner sighed. It would be the last piece of business they could attend to before the carriage rolled away. Or at least that was what Wagner thought at the time. Pinkerton always surprised him.

"Anderson will quit and join the police department if we don't let him go into the field," Wagner replied. "He's young, tough, strong. I think he can handle it. And we'll lose him if we say no."

"Put him with MacNeal," Pinkerton replied.

30   J. D. HARDIN

Before Wagner could acknowledge his superior, the bear of a Scotsman wheeled and got into the coach.

The door closed. The driver urged the team forward. Wagner watched as the carriage began to roll away.

Pinkerton stuck his head out of the window. "You know where to reach me, William."

"Yes, sir!"

"Send me a telegram when you hear from Raider!"

Wagner waved until Pinkerton's head returned to the coach.

When the carriage swung around a corner, he went back inside the office.

Things were more relaxed, but Wagner decided to glare at everyone to let them know that this was not a holiday. They still had to do their work, just as he did. Pinkerton's absence was not an invitation to sloth.

He sat at his desk, trying to focus on his work. But he found himself time and again staring at the front door. What the devil did he think he was waiting for?

Then he remembered Pinkerton's last command.

Wagner was waiting for word from Raider. The big galoot from Arkansas seemed to be the only loose end. And it would be a while before the loose end was finally tied up.

Elk Mountain wasn't much of a town, but Raider still managed to draw a crowd. It started at the edge of the shoddy little burg. One lone man on foot began to follow him. Then two or three more appeared out of nowhere. By the time he arrived at the storefront that was marked "Trader" he had gathered at least ten or twelve residents of Elk Mountain.

They all stood back when Raider dismounted.

He turned toward them, his face begrizzled, his hair thick and matted like a mountain man's scalp. "Any law in this town?"

Someone replied that they didn't even have a town, much less some law.

Raider gestured to the body that was flung over the saddle. "I hear y'all been bothered by this man. Rattler Rogers."

They talked among themselves, whispering and pointing at the body. The crowd had swelled to almost twenty. When the proprietor of the "Trader" store came out, Raider figured to be looking at the entire populace.

"Rattler Rogers," Raider said to the storekeeper.

The man put his hands on his hips. "I heard of him. Didn't figure he'd turn up dead this quick."

"Neither did he," the big man replied.

Raider looked at the citizens before him. He picked the roughest-looking man among them and asked him if he wanted to earn a dollar. All he had to do was watch the body.

The man asked if Raider was a marshal.

"No, I'm a Pinkerton. Now, do you want to earn a dollar or not?"

There were plenty of takers for the dollar, so the man quickly said yes. He took the reins of the dead man's horse and told everyone to stand back. It didn't take him long to enjoy his new authority.

Raider turned back to the storekeeper. "You got any food inside?"

"Stew."

Probably made with horsemeat, Raider thought.

But he went in and stood by a barrel as he wolfed down the plate of stew. It wasn't bad. And the storekeeper gave him some bread to go with it.

Raider asked for whiskey or beer. It didn't matter. The storekeeper was dry. Not even a jug of home squeezings.

"Just my luck," the big man said.

"The whore might have some."

Raider gawked, like he couldn't believe he had heard it. "Whore?"

"Yeah. Lives back behind here in a little shack. Name's Becky. She charges two dollars, so there aren't many customers around here. Don't matter much to her. I don't think she likes whorin' much. She makes enough to pay me rent on the shack."

"And when she don't have the rent, you take it in trade," Raider offered. "You think she's got whiskey?"

The storekeeper was blushing, still embarrassed that Raider had figured out how he got his rent money on the shack. "She keeps a bottle sometimes."

Raider gulped the last bite of bread. "How much I owe you?"

The storekeeper glared at him. "Two dollars!"

"And how much is the whore's rent for a week?"

The man glared at him but replied, "Three dollars."

Raider slapped a ten-dollar gold piece and a silver dollar on the barrel in front of him. "Here's eleven bucks. Two for the stew and three weeks rent for the whore."

"She's still gonna charge you two dollars," the man said.

"I don't care. Just point the way."

"Out back, through that door."

Raider strode toward the doorway, feeling pretty good. Things had worked out better than he could have hoped. At least for the moment. And if the whore had a bottle of whiskey, what more could a man ask for in Elk Mountain, Wyoming?

Raider pulled back the cloth door that covered the entrance of the whore's shack. She started when she saw him standing there. Her lean body was reclining on a brass bed that seemed strangely out of place in the dingy hovel. Her soft white hands held a vanity mirror and a gilded hairbrush. She had been combing long, blond tresses that fell around her white shoulders.

When she was over the shock of Raider's untimely entrance, she quickly went back to looking at herself in the mirror. "Don't you know how to knock?" she said curtly. Her mouth was thick and pouty, rubbed with red rouge.

Raider thought she was a little skinny. Her thin frame was covered by a cotton half-slip and billowing bloomers. Maybe twenty years old, but probably closer to eighteen. Raider just kept staring at her, like he could not believe he had happened on such a delicate creature in Elk Mountain.

The girl lifted her round blue eyes to glare at him. "Did you just come to look, cowboy?"

Raider found himself taking off his hat. "Is your name Becky?"

She hesitated, dropping the brush and the mirror into her lap. "That's me." She sighed. "It's two dollars."

He stepped into the shack, closer to her bed. It was a depressing abode except for the brass bed and the girl who sat on it: a potbellied stove, a plank floor, knotholes in the planked walls.

"Must get cold in here durin' the winter," Raider heard himself saying.

She nodded, chortling ironically. "Cold ain't the half of it. I like to took up with the pneumonia last winter. I even had to go in and sleep with Silas a couple of times."

"Silas?"

"The trader." She exhaled, like she was bored. "What the devil do you want, cowboy?"

He gestured to a rickety wooden chair. "Mind if I take a load off?"

She looked at her pretty moon face in the mirror again. "Suit yourself. It's still two dollars."

"I'll give you twenty," Raider said offhandedly.

Becky's eyes narrowed. "What?"

"Twenty dollars."

She chortled again. "Sure. I've heard that before."

Raider felt mischievous, like he wanted to teach this whore a thing or two. It might be fun. And he had to do something to take his mind off the bodies of those miners. Thank God it was all behind him.

"Twenty dollars," the girl scoffed. "Why the hell would you want to give me twenty dollars?"

Raider kept smiling at her. "Aw, that ain't all I done. I paid three weeks' rent for you."

This time she put her hand on her hip. "The hell you say!"

"Ask Silas."

She still didn't trust him. "Santa Claus don't come till Christmas, cowboy. And I don't care what else you say, I still get two dollars."

What a pretty blond badger she was. Tough as nails. She was too good a whore to be stuck in Elk Mountain.

Raider took his last twenty-dollar gold piece and tossed it on the bed in front of her. "Twenty dollars."

She stared at the double eagle without touching it. "Why you want to give me twenty dollars, cowboy?"

"At two dollars a poke, I oughta be good for ten times. Ten times or other favors."

"Ain't nothin' I got worth twenty dollars. And I ain't gonna let you poke me in the butt. I don't like that."

Raider held out his hands. "Becky, when I walked in here, I knowed right away that you was a first-class lady."

Her face softened a little. "You did?"

He nodded politely, smiling, seized by a sudden impulse to treat her tenderly. "I saw that brass bed and I said 'This girl has got what it takes to be a real fine Louisiana lady.' I mean, any woman who can serve up a brass bed in a place like Elk Mountain has to have somethin' goin' for her."

She put a dainty hand to her throat. "It did take a lot to get this bed. But I got it."

Raider gestured toward her with a gentlemanly wave. "And look at yourself. Why, when I rode into this pigsty, I said to myself, 'There ain't nothin' in this town but dirt and maggots.'"

"You can say that again."

"Then I find you, Becky. You're lyin' back on that bed like the queen of... I don't know what. And I swear that I ain't never seen nobody prettier, not even when I was in New Orleans."

Becky's eyes lit up. "I always wanted to go to New Orleans. Have you really been there?"

"Lotsa times," Raider went on. "Only the whores there are different. They know what a man wants. They treat him like a king. See, only a queen knows how to treat a king. Those high-time ladies never let you think that they don't like you. They always make you feel like some Mississippi Delta daddy. The royal flush or blackjack."

Becky lowered her eyes. "I'm not like those women."

"Sure you are," Raider urged. "Why, you could find a bath and a razor. Then I could have a shave."

"I could cut your hair!" she offered. "I used to do that for my husband before he died. That's how I got stuck here."

Raider nodded appreciatively. "I bet you even got some whiskey," he said slyly. "We could have a few drinks after I clean up."

She perched on the edge of the mattress. "I got half a bottle under my bed. It's real, too. Not home brew."

Raider sighed deeply. "And you said you weren't worth twenty dollars."

Becky picked up the double eagle. "You got yourself a deal, cowboy."

Raider leaned back on Becky's bed. He was naked, still shivering from the cold bath. He had also shaved in cold water. Becky draped a blanket around his shoulders while she trimmed his hair, but that hadn't been enough to ward off the afternoon chill. Clouds had covered the afternoon sky, bringing the threat of rain, or maybe snow.

Becky looked down at him. "Well, you got a big one there."

"Let's get under the covers, honey. I'm cold."

Her face was dour as she stripped down. He wondered what was bothering her. Women could change so quick. Maybe if he didn't ask her, the trouble would simply go away.

Her thin body slid next to his. Raider pulled the blanket over them and wrapped his arms around her. He needed to sleep, but afterward. His manhood had already become engorged with the girl next to him.

He guided her hand down to his prick.

Becky touched him but then pulled back.

"What's wrong?" He had to ask.

She got all teary-eyed. "I ain't never had one that big before. I'm scared that it's gonna hurt me."

He kissed her soft cheek. "I ain't gonna hurt you, punkin. Just do like I say and ever'thing is gonna be all right."

He put her hand back on his cock.

She started to massage the stiff member. He told her to jerk him up and down, like she was shucking corn. Suddenly she was an expert. He figured that she had shucked corn before.

Raider slid his hands down her back, cupping the firm round cheeks of her ass. "Oh yeah, honey, you're too fine to be stuck in Elk Mountain."

Her eyelids had gotten heavy. He felt the warmth that spread through her tender body. She was starting to like it.

Raider parted her thighs, touching the top of her yellow mound. He let his fingers play through the fine hair. No need to rush. Get her going. She'd be better if she was hot.

His fingertips strayed to the fleshy petals of her cunt. He parted the lips, touching her at the top, rubbing the spot that always drove women crazy. A whore had showed him how to do it.

Becky flinched when he touched her there. She tried to take his hand away. Her body was trembling.

"No man ever touched me there," she whispered.

"But you touch it. Don't you?"

She frowned and started to say something.

Raider put a finger to her lips. "Don't be ashamed. All women touch it. Whores more than straight women. But they all touch it."

He put his fingertips to work.

Becky shivered and pushed her thighs together.

Raider parted them again, forcing her to lay back, rubbing her until her teeth were gnashing. "You're ready," he told her, slipping his middle finger into her hot crevice.

Becky writhed with his finger inside her. "I never thought it would feel so good."

She spread her legs, like she wanted him to get on top.

But Raider wasn't ready to give up the game. "Ain't you ever been on top, Becky?"

"What?"

He quickly rolled her over on top of him. "Like this."

She laughed. "Really?"

He shifted around until his cock was between her legs. "Feel it. You're wet, honey. You want it, don't you?"

"Yes, I want it."

She began to move her hips, rubbing her wet cunt against his rigid member.

Raider let her play for a few minutes and then took over again. "Now straddle me. Go on."

She lifted her body, now an eager participant.

"Grab my whanger. Go on."

She took him into her soft hand.

"Now put it where it's supposed to be."

Becky slipped the tip of his cock into the notch of her pussy.

"Do it slow," he said to her. "Take as much as you want."

It took her a while to impale herself. He was surprised when she took it all. She just sat there for a minute, feeling the big thing inside her. Raider prodded her ass a little and she started to move.

Up and down. She took him in and out. So tight. Raider had to hold back. He wanted her to feel it. The shiver.

Her face screwed up in a funny expression. Her lips parted. Her nipples grew tight on the small mounds of her breasts.

Suddenly her body went rigid. A spasm swept over her. Becky collapsed on top of him, writhing on his chest, trying to force her tongue between his lips. She shook like a willow leaf in a sandstorm.

"What happened to me?" she asked.

Raider wasn't sure how to explain it. "You felt it," he told her. "Like lightnin', I reckon. It strikes you but you don't see it."

She rolled off him.

His cock was still pronging to one side.

She wrapped her hand around the base of his prick. "You didn't feel it."

He parted her legs again. "I will."

When he started to roll over on top of her, Becky spread her thighs, no doubt awaiting more pleasures that she had never known before.

He prodded her, pushing against her cunt.

There was a sucking noise as she accepted him.

She was such a wispy little thing. Raider didn't want to hurt her. He started out slow, until it was obvious that she wanted him to pick up the pace.

"I think I'm gonna feel it again," she whispered.

Raider's hips were driving downward. He felt his own climax starting to rise. Her cunt was so damned tight.

"Inside me," she whispered. "Deep."

He collapsed on top of her, pushing his prick to the hilt, discharging his load. Becky gasped, feeling her own release. He left it inside her for a long time, until he started to get drowsy.

He rolled off, pulling the blanket over him. "How 'bout lightin' a fire in that stove?" he told her.

Becky obeyed him almost immediately. She threw kindling into the potbellied stove and tossed a match after it. When the flames swelled inside the stove, she fed bigger logs to the fire.

She came back and knelt by the bed, rubbing Raider's forehead. "I'm in love with you, cowboy. I know it now."

Raider tried to pretend he was asleep.

"You want that whiskey now?" she asked him.

He rolled over, looking at her sweet face. Damn it, maybe he was in love with her, too. And here she was offering some hooch. Hell, a little snort wouldn't hurt before he closed his eyes.

"I'd like a drink, Becky."

She got the bottle from beneath the bed. The whiskey got them going so they humped again. Afterward, Raider was ready for sleep.

Becky lay beside him, stroking his forehead. She felt like a high-class courtesan of the Mississippi Delta. The big man had made her feel that way. Him and his tricks in the bed.

"What's your name, cowboy?"

"Raider."

"Hmm. I like it."

She kept stroking his head.

Raider was afraid she would talk forever. He wanted to tell her to shut up, but somehow he couldn't bring himself to be mean to her. Was that the way you felt about a woman when you loved her?

Becky seemed to be enjoying the sound of her own voice.

"I'm goin' with you when you leave here, Raider."

He hadn't really paid much attention to her last statement. His eyes were closing. He figured she wouldn't go with him when it was time to leave.

He couldn't have been more wrong.

He slept for a while, until Becky screamed.

Then the big man from Arkansas opened his eyes to see a rifle pointed in his face.

There were men outside too, bumping against the shack.

The man with the rifle told him not to move.

Raider stayed still, wondering what the hell was going on.

CHAPTER SIX

At first Raider thought he might be lost in some long, dark dream. But the rifle in front of him was real enough. The man pointed it right at his head. When Raider's eyes finally focused on the rifleman, he saw the tin star inside the open duster.

Two more gunmen backed up the lawman.

There seemed to be several of them at the crude window.

Becky drew the covers around her naked body. She crouched next to Raider, trembling. He sure as hell couldn't save her from the lawman's rifle. The lawman had on the same pointy hat as the rancher who had lent Raider the black stallion.

"I'd say you shouldn't move," the lawman said—if he was a lawman.

Raider stared straight at him. "I ain't goin' nowhere, Sheriff."

"I'm *Marshal* Bick Johnson, from Cheyenne."

"I saw the badge. I just want to know why you drew down on me."

Marshal Johnson gestured with the barrel of a Winchester. "Get out of that rack and put your clothes on."

Becky started to move.

Marshal Johnson tipped his hat to her. "Beggin' your pardon, miss, but if you'd be so kind as to stay in that bed, we'll leave you alone direckly."

Becky put her hand on Raider's shoulder.

He pulled away, swinging his legs over the side of the bed. "That's all right, Becky. Do like the lawman says."

Johnson nodded to Raider. "You'd be smart to do the same."

Raider took a deep breath. "I ain't goin' nowhere, Bick."

The marshal flinched a little. "Do I know you?"

"Not yet."

The big man came off the bed. He saw the Peacemaker on the bedpost. The marshal saw it too.

"Don't think it," Johnson said.

Raider reached for his pants. "That iron ain't in workin' order anyway."

And he had left the damned Winchester on the rancher's horse.

Too many guns outside to try anything just yet.

When he was dressed, the marshal backed out the door, telling Raider to follow. As he moved outside, two men grabbed him and started to tie his hands in front of him. Raider let them. He kept his wrists apart so the ropes would loosen later.

He counted seven guns who rode with Johnson.

Where, and why, had the marshal raised a posse?

When his bonds were secure, Johnson prodded him in the middle of the back, using the Winchester barrel to move him along.

The other men flanked him on both sides as they started to move toward the "Trader" store.

"Mind if I know why you're arrestin' me?" Raider asked.

"You ain't arrested yet," the marshal replied.

They went around the building, coming out in front of the store. Johnson led the big man up to the black stallion and the outlaw's roan. The guard who had Raider's dollar was gone. At least his rifle and his saddlebags were still there. Too careless all at once. He had been so damned tired. But that was no excuse for being stupid.

Johnson moved beside the roan and its dead cargo. "Can you tell me the name of this man?"

WYOMING AMBUSH 41

Raider shrugged. "Rattler. Rattler Rogers. I chased him up here from Kansas. I'm a Pinkerton."

Johnson looked sideways at him. "You sure you ain't Rogers? Killed the Pinkerton and now you're pretendin' to be him?"

Raider gestured to his saddlebags. "I got credentials that say who I am. Have a look-see, Marshal." He grinned disrespectfully. "My agency always wants me to bend for local lawmen."

The marshal dug out the papers and gave them a glance. "I can't read."

One of his posse men stepped up beside him. "I can. Yep, this says he's a Pinkerton. But he could still be Rogers."

Johnson nodded. "That's true. What do you have to say about this, big man? Any answers?"

Raider figured to try the professional approach. "Marshal, I'd be obliged if you'd believe me on this thing. I tracked Rogers to that family's dig down on that creek. I can take you there if—"

"We already been there," the marshal said. "Found three graves. Killed that whole family."

Spectators, who had been gathering steadily, let out a collective sigh for the fallen members of their community.

Raider nodded toward the body. "I caught him about a' hour after he shot 'em. I was the one who buried 'em."

"We were chasin' Rogers too," the marshal offered. "Only we came up through another pass."

Raider figured these dense local boys were missing the point. "Look at him, Marshal. He matches the description I got of Rogers. Blond hair. Check his saddlebags."

Johnson did that immediately. He found the stash of silver that Rattler Rogers had stolen from the dead miners. There was nothing else in the saddlebags. Nothing else pointed directly to Rogers. The outlaw must've emptied them to make room for the silver.

The marshal glared at the tall Pinkerton. "Those miners were robbed. How do I know you aren't somebody who kilt 'em, even kilt Rogers so you could get away with that silver? Then you say you're a Pink till you're out of the territory."

Raider realized the lawman had a point. That would have

been the perfect dodge for a robber. Pose as a lawman or a bounty hunter or a Pinkerton, say you were taking the body back for a reward. Who would doubt you? And who else would transport a corpse *but* a lawman?

"What do you have to say for yourself, sir?" the marshal asked.

Raider sighed, shrugging. "Well, I reckon we got to walk on to the next creek if we're gonna get a drink of water."

Johnson wasn't one to talk in riddles. "Something else, sir. This horse you're ridin' belongs to Mr. William Walters. It has the Double-W brand."

"He loaned it to me himself," Raider started, "if you—"

Somebody in the crowd got excited. "Horse stealin'. That's a hangin'. You hang for horse stealin'!"

The marshal lifted the rifle and fired a quick shot into the air.

Everybody, including Raider, flinched at the sound.

"Nobody's hangin' nobody," Marshal Johnson said.

Raider suddenly felt like the lawman was his best friend. "Johnson, I'm tellin' you, Walters loaned me this mount."

"That's his own private stallion," said one of the posse riders. "I know, worked for Walters for a while."

Johnson eyed Raider again. "He's right. I've seen Walters on this black once or twice. Why'd he give up his mount to you?"

Raider pointed south with his bound hands. "I met him on the range. I helped him kill some wolves, and then I told him I was chasin' Rogers. He said that Wyomin' didn't need no more thievin' sidewinders, so he let me have his horse to chase Rogers."

Johnson surveyed his men. "Anybody know anything about wolves?"

The man who had worked for Walters said that he had heard about a pack of wolves that had been hitting Big Bill's herd.

"There," Raider offered. Then, to the man: "I owe you a drink."

Johnson cogitated for a few moments. Finally he turned to his men. "All right, get your horses. Mount up." He looked at Raider. "And get the Pinkerton on the stallion. Make sure he can hang on to the reins."

Raider held out his hands. "Can you untie me?"

"Not all the way," Johnson replied.

Raider started to protest.

Johnson quickly proved to be a direct man, cutting him off immediately. "Sir, I take you to be who you say you are. But this mount you're ridin' don't belong to you, so I have to take you with me until this matter can be cleared up."

Raider didn't have much choice. He had to keep his mouth shut. Just ride along. Hope like hell that Walters would clear him.

What if Big Bill decided to say that Raider had stolen his mount?

That could mean the fat end of a noose.

Raider wanted to make one more offer to the marshal. "Johnson, when we get to the next wire office, I want you to send a telegram to the Pinkerton National Detective Agency in Chicago, Illinois. William Wagner is the man I work for. He can set you straight."

Johnson had already climbed onto a tall pinto. "Nearest wire is in Cheyenne. Until then, I have to arrest you for horse stealin'."

Two men helped Raider onto the stallion. One of them took the rifle from the scabbard. Raider told him to take care of the '76. The big man didn't figure to be tied up forever.

As the posse started out of town with their prisoners—dead and alive—Raider heard a high voice calling to him. It was Becky. She ran out onto the porch of the general store.

Raider looked over his shoulder to see her waving at him.

"I love you, honey," she called. "I'll see you in Cheyenne."

A few of the posse riders snickered.

Raider just turned his head around, gazing forward, wondering if Becky really meant to follow him.

William Wagner was delighted when the messenger delivered the telegram from Wyoming. The lad said that the key operator had sent it over special-like, as he knew that Wagner was waiting for word from the agent called Raider. Wagner thanked the lad and tipped him a bright penny.

Wagner opened the message, expecting some terse communiqué to signal a successful capture of Raider's quarry. Instead, he read a most unusual request for the big man's services. The sender of the telegram seemed to know Raider's whereabouts, and the completion of the Rattler Rogers case. Why hadn't Raider sent the telegram himself?

Wagner decided to send the reply immediately. He penned the message carefully, saying that Raider could take the case only if he reported back directly to the agency. Under no other circumstances.

Wagner didn't like the feel of the thing. Why hadn't Raider sent in his own message? He decided to take the reply to the Western Union office himself.

The key operator smiled when Wagner walked in. "Another message, sir. About Raider."

Wagner quickly read the operator's scrawled writing. "My God, Raider's in jail. Suspicion of horse stealing."

"You got a reply?" the operator said, his pencil ready.

"Yes," Wagner said angrily. "Two of them!"

Raider lay back in the Cheyenne jail, looking up at the planks on the ceiling. The damned cell was cold inside, especially when the potbellied stove died down. October was here already, bringing the first chills of autumn. Aspens would soon be gold-leaved, and grizzlies would sprout winters coats. Raider thanked the Good Lord for his shearling jacket, otherwise the week-long stay in the jailhouse would have been unbearable.

Johnson and the others had been treating him pretty good. Even on the ride back, which had taken two days, they had been friendly. Johnson fed him twice a day and gave him coffee in the morning. Raider just wished the lawman would hurry up and let him go.

The telegrams had been sent and someone had been dispatched to look for William Walters. Big Bill was supposedly gone on a hunting trip. But he'd turn up sooner or later, Johnson said. The stallion was safe in the livery, and Raider's gear had been stored, the marshal insisted. Johnson also told him that the hammering and sawing outside the window wasn't a gallows, only a porch for the feed and grain store.

Raider figured the lawman would lie to him about a gallows, so he assumed the worst. It drove him crazy sometimes. He wanted to get up and shake the damned bars. Get free.

But he always settled down, praying that justice would tilt the scale his way. Waiting. That was what a good hunter did. Only he wasn't a hunter now. He was prey for the gallows.

That evening, Marshal Johnson came in and slid Raider's dinner under the cell door. "Fried chicken tonight."

"Still no word?" the big man asked.

Johnson shook his head. "Sorry. Somebody said the line is down west of here. Big Bill hasn't turned up yet, but one of his hands said that he did give his horse to somebody."

"Can't you let me out?"

"Not till Walters points a finger and says so himself," Johnson said. "In the meantime, you got a visitor."

Raider squinted at the lawman. "Visitor?"

Johnson went into his office and ushered in a blond-haired girl.

Raider couldn't believe his eyes. "Becky!"

She grinned. "I told you I'd be here."

"How the devil..."

She put her hands on the bars. "I walked part of the way. Then I hitched a ride with a tinker. He wanted me to do it with him, but I wouldn't. I told him I was comin' to Cheyenne to see my man."

Raider sat down and started to eat his dinner.

Johnson stayed close by, to make sure Becky didn't help him escape.

The girl went on and on, talking to everyone and no one at the same time.

Raider still had to take it as a good sign that she had come. What else did he have to make him feel better?

Raider heard voices. He opened his eyes to the bright rays of morning. The stove had died, and it was cold. He could still hear Becky talking, even though the marshal had taken her away the night before.

Was she back already?

No, it was two male voices. He thought he recognized both

of them. One was the marshal, and the other one was . . . Raider sat up quickly.

He heard their boots clomping on the floorboards.

A deep voice resonated through the jailhouse. "You should have seen 'em, Bick. Sheep so big you could ride 'em. They were so purty that I couldn't bring myself to shoot but one. And I only shot that one because I wanted to have it for meat."

Raider saw them come through the door.

"Stand up," the marshal told him.

The big Pinkerton rose to stare at the man in the fur coat.

Johnson gestured toward the prisoner. "That him, Mr. Walters?"

Big Bill squinted at Raider. "Well, it was dark out there, but I think I can vouch for this man. Son, I gave you my horse. The marshal here seems to think you stole it."

Raider shrugged. "Well, Big Bill, you know how lawmen can get. Why, they're as finicky as an old widow sometimes."

Johnson turned his key in the lock. "Sorry, Pinkerton. I just wasn't takin' no chances. By the way, the wire's up. Still no word from your people, Raider, but the Kansas marshal says we can bury Rogers for you."

Raider stepped out of the cell. "Thanks. Where's my guns?"

Big Bill looked anxiously at the big man. "Aw, Raider, you ain't gonna cause trouble, are you?"

"No, I just want my guns."

Johnson started for his office. "All of your gear is out front. Come on."

True to the marshal's word, Raider's belongings were stacked neatly in the corner. His saddle had been soaped and cleaned. His Winchester and Colt were right there beside his saddlebags. Both guns were shiny.

"I had your pistol fixed," the marshal offered. "Big Bill brought in your saddle when he got word that you were here."

Raider exhaled. "Well, Johnson, I don't reckon I can stay too mad at you. Not after this."

"Just try to see my side of it," the marshal said. "Wyomin' is a tough place. Sometimes men ain't who they say they are."

Big Bill spoke up, laughing at Johnson. "But we're gonna stop all that, ain't we, Marshal? All we have to do is get Wyomin' into the Union. Then a lot of our troubles'll be over."

Raider picked up his gunbelt and strapped it around his hips. He checked the Peacemaker, dry-firing it. The spring had been fixed, just like the marshal had said. He was already beginning to forget about the seven days in jail.

Big Bill clapped Raider on the shoulder. "Son, I'd like to invite you up to my lodge for some good food, some whiskey, and maybe some deer huntin'."

Raider shook his head. "Sorry, I got to stay here and wait for word from my agency."

Big Bill smiled, like he was Raider's favorite uncle or something. "Look here, I'll leave one of my men in town. He can ride up as soon as any word comes through for you."

"I don't know, Walters."

Big Bill kept grinning. "Look here, I just cleared you. Now I want to make it up to you, after you shot them wolves and spendin' the week in jail. All 'cause I wasn't here to speak up for you."

Raider hesitated for a moment. "You say you got whiskey?"

"All the way from across the ocean," Walters replied. "I prefer an Irish blend myself."

"I'd only be able to stay for a couple of days," Raider replied. "Even if word don't come from my boss, I still have to move on."

Walters shrugged. "You're a free man, sir. But I would be grateful if you'd accept my hospitality."

"He makes good barbecue, Pinkerton," the marshal chimed in. "Best smokehouse I ever seen."

How could Raider say no?

"I still don't have a horse," he said. "And I don't have any money till my agency sends my back pay."

The marshal spoke to that matter. "Take any horse you want in the livery. Kansas is sendin' a reward this way, for Rattler. I'll pay for your mount out of that."

Raider picked up his saddle. "Since you put it that way, Big Bill, let's ride. I ain't had any good barbecue in a dog's age."

Walters laughed loudly. "Learned how to make smoke meat when I was runnin' Yankee supplies through Rebel territory."

Johnson squinted at the burly man. "Which side you fight for, Walters?"

"Whichever one paid me."

They all laughed again.

Raider started out into the street.

Walters came after him. "You got long legs, big man."

The rancher followed alongside Raider until they had cleared the marshal's office.

Then he tried to stop him. "Pinkerton!"

He turned to look at Walters. "Yeah?"

The rancher moved closer, leaning in. "Listen, I didn't want to say anythin' in front of the marshal"—he unfolded a piece of paper—"but I sent a telegram to your agency myself."

Raider nodded appreciatively. "Much obliged. It's always better to have somebody else to clear your name when you're in a jam."

Big Bill shook his head. "No, that's not what I wanted to do. I sent the telegram from Laramie a day after I gave you my horse. They said it might take a couple of days to get through, and I still haven't got a reply."

"Why'd you send it, then?"

"I want you to come to work for me," the rancher replied. "But I don't want to talk about it now."

"Why not?"

Big Bill looked to both sides. "Because I don't know who else is listenin'. Come on, let's go get you a horse."

Walters urged him toward the livery.

Raider tried to press the man for an answer, but Big Bill wouldn't tell him why he wanted to hire a Pinkerton. So he just shut up. He knew the rancher would make himself clear in his own time. It wasn't gentlemanly to be huffy with somebody who had invited you to dinner.

At the stable, Raider chose a strong-looking roan. As he was saddling up, he noticed that Big Bill had already saddled the stallion. The black looked ready to run.

"Fine horse," Raider offered.

Big Bill nodded. "Wouldn't trade him for all the tea in China."

Raider knew about tea and China, but he couldn't think of anything smart to say. "Well, thanks anyway for lettin' me borrow him."

The liveryman wanted to know how Raider was going to pay for the roan. He told the man about the deal with the marshal's office, and Big Bill backed him up. The stableman said that Raider shouldn't ride out until he could clear it with the marshal.

Raider said he'd wait.

When the liveryman was gone, Raider turned to Big Bill. "Walters, you sure you don't want to tell me what's botherin' you? I mean, is it really that bad?"

Big Bill exhaled his dejection. "If I'm right, Raider, this thing is gonna be a whole lot worse'n them wolves we shot."

Raider was tactful, but he still couldn't get the man to talk. He knew he had to trust Walters, at least for a while. After all, Big Bill had freed him from the territorial jailhouse, not to mention giving him the horse when Raider really needed it.

The liveryman came back in. "Okay, you can take the roan. And Mr. Walters, there won't be any charge on the black. Not from you, anyways. The marshal will take care of that."

Big Bill looked at Raider. "I wonder how big a reward there was on Rattler Rogers?"

Raider waved him off. "Lawmen take rewards, not Pinkertons. If Johnson can live with it, I can live without it."

Walters laughed again. "Doggone it, Raider, I think you and me are gonna be friends before this is over."

The big man shrugged. "We'll see."

They led their mounts into the street.

Raider had one foot in the stirrup when he heard the woman screaming. He looked up the street to see Becky running at him. He frowned and looked away. He had forgotten all about her.

"Who's that?" Walters asked.

"Somebody I ain't ready to see," Raider replied. "She followed me here from Elk Mountain."

"Pretty little thing," the rancher offered. "Blond hair and all."

Becky ran up and threw her arms around Raider's waist. "I thought they'd never let you out."

Raider pushed her away, gently but firmly. "Honey, you can't follow me all over the place."

"But I love you," Becky said. "And you love me!"

Big Bill was gaping at her, smiling.

Raider took her to one side. "Becky, you can't come with

me. I'm a Pinkerton. Sometimes people try to kill me. If you come along, you could be killed too."

"I don't care, as long as I can come with you."

She had such an innocent expression on her face that he couldn't bring himself to get rough with her. "Honey, I—"

"Raider, the way you diddled me back in Elk Mountain . . ." She smiled at him, breaking his heart. "Nobody ever did me like that. And I know you love me. You have to."

Big Bill swung into the saddle behind them. "Time's a-wastin', Raider. If she wants to come along, bring her. There's plenty of room at my lodge."

Raider turned to glare at the rancher.

Becky rushed past him, wrapping her arms around Big Bill's leg. "Thank you. Thank you. I'll be good. I can cook and clean."

Raider shook his head. "Big Bill, I don't think . . ."

Walters smiled at him. "What could it hurt? Hell, she can ride with me. This black will carry both of us."

He put down a hand for Becky.

When she grabbed his wrist, he pulled her onto the saddle with him.

"Thank you," she said again, wrapping her arms around Big Bill.

Raider thought they were funny-looking together—Bill in his fur coat and Becky in her calico dress. "I still don't think we oughta let her come with us," he offered one more time. "Women can be a lot of trouble."

Walters looked over his shoulder. "You won't be any problem, will you, Becky?"

"No, Daddy."

Raider flinched. She had really called him *daddy*. He hoped Big Bill wasn't making a terrible error in judgment.

Raider swung into the saddle of his new mount.

"Don't worry, Pinkerton," Big Bill said, "Ever'thin' is gonna be all right."

"It's your ranch," Raider replied. "You can invite whoever you want."

With that, they both spurred their mounts and headed away from Cheyenne, taking the blond-haired girl with them.

CHAPTER SEVEN

They rode for a long time, until it was well past dark. Then they kept on riding for another long time, into the first hours of the morning. Raider was glad that Big Bill seemed to know his way around, so he let the rancher take the lead. Walters held steady, bouncing along with the girl riding behind him. Raider still couldn't bring himself to feel good about having Becky along. Her arrival was no longer a good omen.

Big Bill slowed his mount when they neared the river. Raider fell in beside him. The roan was holding up as good as the stallion. Both horses started to walk parallel to the stream.

Walters pointed to vague shadows across the river. "Right over there was where we killed those wolves."

Raider just nodded, feeling a shiver down his spine.

Becky opened her eyes behind Big Bill. "Wolves?"

Walters laughed. "Don't you worry, honey. Me and Raider done killed 'em all. They won't hurt you."

He winked at Raider, who shook his head. "How much farther?"

"Not long," Walters replied. "We'll walk these animals for

a spell and then water 'em. Shouldn't be more'n another hour or two."

Raider glanced up at the clear sky. "After midnight, ain't it?"

The rancher took out a pocket watch. "One o'clock."

"Still not that cold for this time of year."

"Gonna get a lot colder," the rancher replied.

Raider felt ready for a bed. The time in jail had made him weak. Might take him a while to get his strength back. He'd just have to gut it out till he was his old self again.

By the time they reached Big Bill's lodge, the moon had risen behind them, casting an eerie light on the rolling plain. Raider could see the mountains now, not in the distance, but high overhead in front of him.

Walters's lodge was right at the base of a steep slope. Raider couldn't see the cattle, but he could hear them all around, bawling, shuffling in the night away from the sounds of two riders. He also detected the levering of a rifle as they reined up in front of a high porch on the front of the lodge.

"That you, Mr. Walters?"

Big Bill dismounted. "It's me, Shorty."

"Who's that with you?"

"Guests of mine, Shorty. That's all you need to know."

He helped Becky out of the saddle.

The girl rubbed her eyes. "Are we here?"

"Yes, darlin'," Big Bill replied.

Raider dropped down from the back of the roan. "Where we s'posed to put our mounts?"

Walters looked up at the sentry on the porch. "Shorty, you take our mounts out to the barn. See that Pepe rubs 'em down and gets 'em fed."

"Yes, sir."

Raider grabbed his Winchester and his saddlebags then gave the reins of the roan to the man called Shorty, who led both mounts away.

Big Bill stepped onto the porch, leading Becky beside him. "Come on, let's all get some sleep."

Raider was right behind him. "I thought we was gonna talk, Walters?"

"Tomorrow."

When they were inside, Walters lit a match and torched the wick of an oil lamp. Raider took in the lodge for the first time. It had been constructed from thick cedar timbers, which were straight and even. Mounted heads of deer, sheep, antelope, buffalo, and elk hung on the walls—one of each. Indian blankets served as tapestries. A tall stone hearth took up most of one wall. Bear rugs and wooden tables. Skins had also been arranged in a circle in the middle of the main parlor, like a tribal meeting place of some Indian council.

Becky's eyes were wide. "Gosh, I never saw anything like this before."

"Well, you can see it better tomorrow," Big Bill said in a fatherly tone. "Now it's time for you to go up top and get some sleep."

Walters pointed to a set of steps that led up to a loft.

Becky broke away from him and slipped next to Raider. "I'm sleepin' with my man tonight," she insisted.

Big Bill shrugged. "Suit yourself. There's two rooms in the loft. I got a bed in the back here. And I'm gonna get in it."

Walters lit another oil lamp and started out of the main parlor. "Good night, all. See you in the mornin'."

When the old gent was gone, Raider glared at Becky. "Did you have to go and say that in front of him?"

She began to pout. "Well, I'm in love with you and—"

Raider gently pushed her away from him. "Honey, we can't be in love. You hear me? Now you ain't sleepin' with me tonight. It ain't respectful to Big Bill. And I might be workin' for him soon enough."

Becky pulled away from him and ran up the stairs, crying.

Raider exhaled defeatedly. They always cried when it got too tough for them. Oh well, he hadn't invited her along. Maybe she'd take up with Big Bill if she stayed around long enough.

He hoisted his gear and went up the steps, taking the room next to Becky. Big Bill had it set up right, a thick mattress on the floor with skins and blankets for cover. It didn't take Raider long to settle down in the warm bed.

His eyes were closing as the footsteps pattered toward him.

He didn't have to look.

He could smell her perfume.

Becky slipped under the covers with him. "I ain't sleepin' alone," she told him. "I don't care if you are mad at me."

Before he could protest, she grabbed him and began the corn shucking movement. His cock swelled, even after the long ride. He rolled over to get closer to her. She began to give him sweet kisses.

"Becky..."

"Oh, hush up, Raider."

She rolled over on top of him, just like he had taught her.

"Becky..."

He felt the moistness of her cunt against his shaft.

"I missed you," she whispered. "When I saw you in that jail, I just wanted to get in that cell with you and tear your pants off."

"Yeah, I..."

She raised up, throwing off the covers, straddling him.

Her soft hand guided the end of his prick to her cunt.

Becky gasped when she felt him there. She started to take him in, sinking slowly onto his prick. When he was all the way inside her, a shiver played through her delicate body.

"Touch my titties," she told him.

Raider felt the erect nubs of her nipples beneath his fingertips.

Becky shook, bobbing up and down, releasing herself with one burst after another. Raider held on, watching, touching her breasts. She had damned sure turned into a spitfire.

"I'm feelin' it," she moaned. "I'm really feelin' it."

She collapsed on top of him, licking his lips.

Raider's stiff manhood was still inside her, throbbing, aching for release.

She looked into his eyes. "You ain't finished."

"I'm gonna get on top," he told her.

She put her fingers on his lips. "No. I want to do it some other way. But not in the butt. I don't like it in the butt."

"I ain't much on that myself," Raider replied. "But I do know a way. Here, get on all fours like a doe."

She hurried to obey him.

He got on his knees and gazed down at her skinny white ass.

Becky parted her legs a little. "Don't hurt me."

"I won't."

He prodded her backside, found the open folds of her cunt, and pushed in the head.

Becky groaned. "More."

He buried himself to the hilt in her.

She rocked back, crying out, moving with him.

"Inside me," she said. "Inside me."

Raider felt his sap rising. He felt her trembling. His release came deep within her. Becky collapsed, falling on her stomach, pulling away from him. Raider was still dripping when he fell beside her.

She tried to catch her breath. "I never knew a man could fuck me like that. I never figured I'd enjoy it so much."

Raider closed his eyes. He was afraid she would start talking again. But pretty soon they were both snoring under the covers.

And when he woke up to all the commotion, Becky was no longer there.

Raider heard the voices of men. He sat up, gazing at the bright cedar walls of the loft. Too much light in the room for it to be early morning. How long had he been sleeping?

Someone was coming up the steps.

Raider reflexively grabbed the Peacemaker that was always at arm's reach.

Big Bill gawked when he rushed in to see the pistol pointed at him.

"Sorry, Walters. Just a habit." He lowered the weapon.

Big Bill had a piece of paper in his hand. "This came for you. It's from your boss—Wagner. It says that you can accept my case, but you have to report in to him first."

Raider's eyes narrowed. "Your man rode all the way out here this mornin' from Cheyenne?"

"It's after noon," Walters replied. "And this message came from Laramie, not Cheyenne. It's a shorter ride. Came in first thing this mornin', and my hand was there to fetch it."

Raider stretched. "I shouldna slept so long."

"Well!" Walters cried. "What's it gonna be? You gonna sign on with me, Raider, or do I have to hire somebody else?"

"First off, Walters, I don't have to work for you if I don't want to. You ain't even told me what you want. And I still have to check in with Wagner."

"My hand can run the message back to Laramie."

Raider waved at the rancher. "Slow down, hoss. We can work all that out later. But right now I got to put some clothes on and maybe have me a cup of hot coffee if you got one."

Realizing that he had reached a stone wall, Walters simply nodded his head. "All right. And there's food if you want it."

"I'll be at the table as soon as I can put on my boots."

Walters turned to go.

"Big Bill?"

He looked back at Raider. "Yeah?"

"For what it's worth, I like you. And if there's somethin' I can help you with, I'll most likely do it. But the agency and me both got particulars. There's just some things we won't throw in with. You get me?"

Walters nodded. "Sorry, I didn't mean to be so bullheaded."

Raider frowned. "Speakin' of bull-headed, where's Becky?"

Big Bill smiled a little. "Oh, I think you're gonna be surprised at Miss Becky. She done run off my squaw, the one I had cookin' for me. Now she's in the kitchen."

"You can have her, Walters. I'll work for free if you get her to marry you."

Big Bill said he would take it into consideration.

Becky was a terror in the kitchen. She had plates heaped full with smoked meat, eggs, biscuits, potatoes, onions, and gravy. As Raider dug in, she went on about cooking for "her man." It made the big man nervous to hear such talk, but he still could not bring himself to be rotten to her, especially with Big Bill at the table. Walters seemed to adore the girl, and she liked him as well.

"More coffee?" she asked them.

They both wanted their cups filled.

Raider swirled his last biscuit in the gravy. "Sure is good, Becky. Why'd you let me sleep so long?"

She ran a hand through his hair. "You just looked so handsome with your eyes closed."

Raider gently pushed her hand away. "Honey, I got to talk to Mr. Walters. Ain't there someplace else you can go for a while?"

Becky started to pout. "Raider..."

Big Bill headed her off. "Becky, why don't you run out to the smokehouse and see how Pepe's doin' with that sheep I gave him to smoke."

She put her nose in the air. "I think I will!"

When she was gone, Raider shook his head. "She's gonna be trouble."

Walters laughed. "Kinda young, but I wouldn't pass her up. I'm lookin' for a wife. That's part of why I came back to Wyomin'. Find me a little lady, have me a son. I'm only forty-five. I got a few good years left."

Raider wanted to be friendly. "Hell, you seem pretty tough to me."

Walters's face grew serious. "Raider, it's about time I told you what's goin' on around here. You want some hooch for that coffee?"

It was still too early for Raider. "Maybe after a while."

Big Bill got up and went to a kitchen cabinet. He brought a bottle back to the table, pouring clean Irish whiskey into his cup. Raider decided it wasn't really that early so he relented and had a snort himself.

The liquor seemed to bring a sad expression to Big Bill's face. "I know I waited a long time to settle down," the rancher started. "Hell, I reckon I just kept thinkin' that I'd die. 'Specially durin' the war."

Raider leaned back, sipping at the spiked coffee, wondering if the story was going to be a long one.

"I made my money," Walters said. "And I ain't always proud of the way I made it. I know I joked about workin' for both sides, blue and gray. But I really did walk the fence. I never had much loyalty to either side after a while. Just boys in uniform who seemed to need what I was sellin'."

Raider shrugged. "Man does what he has to."

"I did just that. But no more, you ain't the kind of man who likes to trifle. Let me get to it."

He stood up, ready for the speech.

Raider took the bottle and poured himself another drink of whiskey.

The rancher started in with his deep voice. "Raider, I care about two things in this life. My ranch and the territory of Wyomin'. When I came back here, I said that I would have a big spread of cattle and that I would work hard to see that Wyomin' becomes a state in the Union."

"Seems likely that the territory'll be a state one of these days," Raider offered. "Colorado got statehood a few years back, so it seems to be spreadin' this way."

Walters grimaced. "Can't be so sure about that, Raider. There's some folks hereabouts these days that don't want to see Wyomin' admitted to the Union. They want to see the territory broken up, give the land to the surroundin' states and territories."

Raider squinted at the rancher. "The hell you say. I ain't heard a thing about that."

"Believe it," Walters went on. "And that's one of the reasons I need your help, Raider."

The big man showed his palms to the rancher. "Whoa, Big Bill, I can't get involved with nothin' like statehood. That's strickly stump-thumpin' politick stuff. You don't want me."

"You won't be involved in my push for statehood," Walters replied. "I just want you to protect me, be my bodyguard."

Raider leaned forward. "You're in danger?"

Big Bill nodded. "Several threats have been made against me. I found steers dead on the range. The words 'Get Out Now' were written in blood on the ground next to the animals."

That got Raider's attention. "You weren't really out there lookin' for wolves, were you, Walters?"

"Well, I knew there were wolves around," the rancher replied. "But I also knew somebody might be gunnin' for me. So we were ridin' patrols for a while. When I found out you were a Pinkerton, I went to Laramie and sent word to your agency that I wanted to hire you. I told them that you had already caught Rattler Rogers, even though you really hadn't, not yet anyway. I wanted to make sure you stayed around."

Raider looked sideways at him. "You didn't make me wait in that jail, did you?"

"Not deliberately. When word finally came that you were

in Cheyenne, I hurried to get there. I was glad to vouch for you because I wanted you to work for me. How 'bout it?"

Raider waved him off. "Let's keep talkin'. You really think somebody's gonna try to kill you?"

Walters sighed. "I'm not sure. At first I thought somebody was tryin' to cover for rustlin'. Make it look like the threats were the work of those who don't want to see Wyomin' become a state of the Union. Now I'm not so sure. Word gets around, and some say that I'll be hurt if I continue to work for statehood. It might be just rumors, but a man starts to thinkin' sometimes."

Raider leaned back again. "Have you lost a lotta cattle?"

Big Bill shrugged. "Maybe twenty head. I got more'n five hundred cows out there, but I hate to lose any of 'em. Winter'll get at least half, and then some'll just up and die on you. That's ranchin'."

Raider grimaced at him. "Is statehood really that big a deal? I mean, most people west of the Mississippi want statehood for their territories."

"Some think that the population of this area is too small to justify makin' it a state. And there is a real move to break it up, give it to the neighbors. But I hope to fight that."

"And you think you need me for protection?" the big man asked.

Walters was about to reply when Becky came in from outside. "Gosh," she told them, her blue eyes wide. "That's the biggest smokehouse I ever seen. And it's full of meat. Pepe says that you need to shoot another deer, though. We're almost out of venison."

Raider smiled at the way she said "we" to Big Bill.

Already settling in.

Nesting.

Becky went on and on, rattling to the breeze.

Raider looked at Big Bill. "What are we gonna do, Walters? She may never stop talkin'."

Walters grinned. "We do what my daddy used to do."

"What's that?"

"We go huntin', Raider. Women hate huntin'."

Becky glared at them. "You're darned right we do! Now get out of this kitchen before I hit you with a rollin' pin!"

She didn't have to tell them twice.

Big Bill led Raider through the lodge, to a private room in the back. The walls of the den were racked with all different kinds of firearms: rifles, shotguns, pistols; flintlocks, breechloaders, double-barrels, repeaters, cartridge-chambered, percussion capped. Raider figured there must've been a hundred weapons on the walls.

"Good job, Walters. This is a bear of a collection."

The rancher was glaring at him. "What about it, Raider? You gonna work for me?"

Raider smiled. "Can I tell you later, after I have time to study on it?"

"All right," Walters replied. "You have until the end of our hunting party."

Raider said that would be plenty of time.

Big Bill was crouched low at the top of a rise, peering down at something. He waved his hand at Raider, indicating that the big man should come up to the crest of the ridge. Raider stepped carefully to where Big Bill was resting, gazing down at the herd of mule deer.

It was almost dark. They had been tracking the herd most of the afternoon, trying to get in a good position for an upwind shot. Now it looked like they had found what they had come after.

Big Bill kept his voice low. "Nice herd."

Raider nodded. He was carrying his '76 Winchester. Big Bill had a long-barreled Sharps .50 caliber.

"Looks like your shot, Big Bill. Those deer are too far for my rifle. I'd never get 'em."

The rancher offered Raider the Sharps. "Go on. It shoots a little to the left. Aim in front of the leg."

Raider smiled at him. "You wouldn't be givin' me a shot so you could talk me into takin' your case."

"That's egg-zackly why I'm doin' it. Now go on."

Raider rested the barrel of the Sharps on the ridge. He flipped up the sight and looked toward the herd. A big buck had his nose to the wind. Would Raider be able to get off the shot before they ran?

"Don't take the buck," Walters said. "Not the big one.

Take the one in the back. He looks old. The wolves would just get him anyway."

Raider didn't argue. He took aim on the scrawny buck in the back and squeezed the trigger. The gun exploded, scaring the herd into a run.

The scrawny buck ran with them.

"Damn," Raider said. "I missed."

Big Bill was staring toward the herd. "Wait a minute."

Raider turned in time to see the scrawny buck falling to the ground, dead on the plain.

"You got him," Walters said. "He just didn't know it."

They mounted their horses and rode after the buck.

Raider watched as Walters skinned out the animal. "You do that pretty good, Big Bill."

The rancher laughed. "You oughta see them wolves. Why, this time next year, I'll have me a wolf coat."

Raider exhaled. "Dog me if this ain't pretty country. I like that little nip in the air. Course, I won't like it when the snow's asshole-deep on a tall mule skinner."

Walters kept on laughing.

When the buck was dressed, they wrapped up the hide and the meat and headed back to the lodge.

They delivered the meat and the hide to Pepe, who looked more Indian than Mexican. Becky had been right. It was a big smokehouse.

By the time they entered the kitchen, the blond-haired cook chided them for being late for dinner.

Both of them feigned hangdog looks of remorse. They sat down to a big dinner of meat, potatoes, gravy, and biscuits. Raider had to admit that Becky could cook. And she was good under the covers. She would have made any man a good wife.

"I do enjoy cookin' for my man," she said, smiling at Raider.

"Why don't we have some whiskey by the fire," Walters said quickly.

Raider joined the rancher in front of the stone hearth. They sat with cups of hooch, looking into the flames. Raider figured it was time for Walters to have his answer.

"I like you, Big Bill. And I want to help you out. I can be your bodyguard. I can find out who made them threats. I'll see if I can find the man who's been stealin' your cows. But that's it. I can't help you with your politickin'. I can't do nothin' that goes against the law or the rules of my agency. You hear me?"

Walters nodded. "Fine by me. I'll have one of my hands run the reply over to the telegraph in Laramie. You can write whatever you want. And I'll pay for it."

"Send a man who can't read nor write," Raider said.

"Why?"

"That way, he can't change nothin' I write."

The rancher nodded appreciatively. "I reckon you Pinks are as smart as they say."

"Smarter, Walters." He pointed a finger at the man. "And I don't care who I'm workin' for. The truth is the only important thing to me. It don't matter to me who falls by the wayside. Rich or poor, high and mighty, or low and dirty. I don't put up with much nonsense."

Big Bill said that was fine with him. Anything Raider needed, just as long as he did his job. Walters swore he didn't have anything to hide.

Raider was about to reply when he heard Becky coming. "I better get up to bed."

Walters chuckled as Raider started for the loft.

"Promise to marry her," he called to Big Bill. "If she says no, tell her you'll buy her a ring."

But it didn't work.

Becky was in bed with him in less than an hour.

She knew what to do now, so there was no stopping her.

He rolled over on top of her, giving her what she wanted.

They fell asleep together.

When Raider awoke the next morning, she wasn't beside him.

He could smell breakfast cooking.

Best to start the case, even if he didn't know what the hell he was going to do with the persistent blond-haired woman.

CHAPTER EIGHT

When Raider dressed, he realized that his jeans and his shirt were a little damp. Had Becky found time to wash them? How late had he slept?

His vest was clean and shiny, his boots buffed to a fine sheen, his Stetson dusted, new socks. Becky had probably talked Walters out of the socks. Raider was just going to have to be firm with her.

But as he sat at the kitchen table, Becky turned and smiled. Her face was rosy, her lips were parted in a grin. She put his breakfast in front of him, and he couldn't think of a thing to say.

"Eat," she said, "then I'll shave you."

"Shave me?"

"You want to look good, don't you?" She patted his shoulder. "Did you like your clean clothes?"

"They're finally dryin' out," he replied. "You didn't have to do that."

She kissed him lightly on the cheek. "Nothin's too good for my man."

"Becky..."

But all he could do was eat. She had made scrambled eggs with smoked meat and onions mixed in. Biscuits with butter and jelly. Raider ate everything and washed it down with half a pot of coffee.

He leaned back from the table. "Where's Big Bill?"

"At the stable. He's makin' sure your roan is ready to ride."

Raider got up. "Well, I better go check on it," he said and started for the door.

"Raider?"

"Yeah?" he said it without looking back.

"When will you be home for dinner?"

What could he say?

He went out of the lodge, hoping that he hadn't hurt her feelings too much. But he wasn't going to answer to any woman. It wasn't his nature. And he knew that he couldn't go against his own grain. Swimming upriver didn't appeal to the big man from Arkansas, even though he found himself in the swift current, battling upstream time after time.

Big Bill was at the corral, watching Pepe working on the shoe of the roan. "Be ready in a minute," he said as Raider stepped up next to him.

Raider nodded. "Roan looks good."

"You can take the stallion if you want," Big Bill said.

"No thanks. I ain't wantin' to get put in jail again. The roan will do. It seems strong enough."

Big Bill reached into his pants pocket. "Here."

He held out five double eagles to Raider.

The big man squinted at the money. "What's that for?"

"Expenses," Walters replied.

Raider took the five golden coins. "I'll pay you back when I get my wages from the agency."

Walters said that would be fine. "Raider, my man is ready to take your telegraph message to Laramie."

Raider shook his head. "Won't have to do it, Walters. I'm goin' there myself. There's some things I gotta do."

Walters frowned. "Like what?"

"Like my business."

"I did hire you to protect me," the rancher said.

Raider chortled. "Hell, Big Bill, you got enough guns here to defeat the cavalry. Bring in some men and put 'em up top, on the roof. Keep your lookouts posted. You'll be as safe as a prairie dog in the middle of a cactus patch."

Walters eyed him. "What you got in mind?"

"Business, Walters. And I aim to get to it."

He started back to the house for his guns.

The ride to Laramie was less than half a day.

Raider rode past the fort, where the blue-coated soldiers were quartered. It always bothered Raider that he had never become a soldier. Although being a Pinkerton was sort of like serving in the Army. Pinkerton and Wagner were his commanders. And he was something of a one-man force.

Laramie was a rough enough town that he didn't attract much attention as he headed down the dusty street.

He passed the saloon, which had already opened its doors for the day.

Raider figured to be in the barroom as soon as he sent the telegram to Wagner. He'd find out what he wanted to know in the saloon. He'd have to be careful, not drink too much. But it could work if he did it right.

He tied his horse in front of the telegraph office.

The key operator looked up and smiled when Raider walked in. "May I help you, sir?"

Raider was suddenly glad that Becky had forced him to spruce up. It might make things easier in the saloon. But he'd send the message first.

He wrote it down. *On job for local man. Last job over. Raider.*

"Send this to William Wagner, Fifth Avenue, Chicago, Illinois."

The key operator nodded. "That'll be two dollars."

"You got room for a double eagle?"

The man frowned. "My, no. It's been a slow day."

Raider shrugged. "Let Wagner pay for it at the other end."

"Very well, I'll send it collect."

The big man smiled, thinking he had pulled one over on Wagner. The smart-alecky ramrod of the Pinkerton Agency would grimace at having to pay for the message. Probably take it out of Raider's back pay.

"Add this," Raider said. " 'Send back wages.' You can hold it for me till I get back, can't you?"

The operator nodded, saying, "There will be an access charge."

"Hell," Raider said, "I don't care. Just hold it. I'll see you in a week. That okay?"

"Fine, sir."

Raider left the telegraph office, heading for the saloon. He had deliberately omitted the name of the agency on the wire to Wagner. He figured the wire office in Chicago knew Wagner well enough to get the message to him. No sense in telling the whole damned territory that he was a Pinkerton agent.

He walked along the sidewalk that led to the saloon. Several ladies who passed smiled at him. He tipped his hat politely and walked on. Probably wives of the officers from the fort, he thought. Nowadays, the Army let their top brass bring their wives along. Hell, the Indians were gone for the most part, so there wasn't any real danger.

The saloon was almost empty.

Two men nursed shots of whiskey at the bar.

Raider pushed through the doors, declaring, "Glory be, this place ain't got nothin' on a graveyard."

The bartender, a red-eyed man looked up at him. "Still early, stranger. What's your pleasure?"

Raider slapped a double eagle on the table. "Your best whiskey. A bottle. And pour one for my friends here."

The barflies looked suspicious at first, but after a couple of snorts they loosened up. Started talking. A few more men came in. They also drank from Raider's bottle. By late afternoon, the big handsome man who was buying drinks had drawn something of a crowd. It was then that he found out what he needed to know.

Raider lifted his own glass, which had been half full for a long time. "To Wyomin'," he said with a mock toast. "Here's hopin' she'll be a state someday."

He watched the reaction of the ten or so men who were surrounding him.

They all cheered and downed their drinks.

"Glad to see y'all are for statehood," Raider went on.

"We can't wait to join the Union," the bartender said. "But it's gonna be a long fight."

"Some say they want to break up the territory and pass it around the horn," Raider said. "Give it to the borderlands."

"Never!" somebody cried.

Shouts of protest.

"Union once and for all!"

Raider lifted his glass again. "To the great state of Wyomin'!"

More cheers.

Raider bought another bottle and passed it around. He had drunk very little himself. It was getting dark outside. He had to make a choice. Where to go next?

He decided to try Rock River.

Raider had been pleased with the reaction of the men in Laramie. They had all seemed unanimously in favor of statehood for Wyoming. Why wouldn't they want to join the Union?

Still, he had to keep things in perspective. One barroom full of men didn't necessarily represent the whole territory. So he'd hit the countryside, the smaller places. Poke around. See what floated to the top.

He rode out of Laramie, heading back east, toward Rock River. Marshal Johnson had taken him through the small settlement on their trip south, when Raider had been in custody. He would be able to find it again, but not in the dark.

Since he didn't want to go back to the ranch to face Becky, he decided to camp after nightfall. He built a fire and curled up in his bedroll. The sky was clear and seemed so close that he could reach up and grab a handful of stars. How could anything be wrong in the world on a night like this?

He slept soundly, waking to the snorts of the roan.

Raider opened his eyes to a terrible sight.

Four Indians stood around him, all holding breech-loader rifles.

Raider's black eyes focused on the one in front of him.

Crow, he thought.

Would they try to hurt him?

Raider slowly stood up. If they had wanted him dead, they would have already shot him. He saw that they had cows with them. Then he noticed the brand on the rump of one steer. A Double-W symbol had been burned into the animal's hide. They had raided Walters's ranch for the beef.

They only had three steers with them.

Raider smiled and nodded at the one in front of him. "How do?"

The man wore a stony expression on his well-lined face. "Tell Walters that we take no more cows. We go north to reservation."

"All right," Raider replied. "Who should I say sends word?"

The Crow warrior, ancient and defeated, waved his arm. "I am Dark Hawk. Tell Walters my son, Half Eagle, not go north."

Raider's eyes narrowed. "Half Eagle?"

Without another word, the Indians turned and started off on foot, driving the steers in front of them.

Raider felt his stomach churning.

He looked to the east, where the sun was edging up over the horizon.

Best to move on and head for Rock River.

On the trail, he kept thinking about the old Indian. Why had Dark Hawk given that strange message for Walters? Maybe he figured the information about Half Eagle was worth a few cows.

Walters hadn't mentioned anything about Indians. Maybe he didn't figure that a few old Crows had the guts to filch cows from his herd. With all the red men moving north, to Canada or reservations, nobody thought much about them anymore.

It made Raider sort of sad when he pondered on it. So he didn't think about it, except to figure that he had solved the problem of Walters's rustlers. Although that really didn't explain who had written "Get Out Now" in blood next to a dead animal. Maybe the Indians had been trying to throw any investigation off track. Dark Hawk had spoken pretty good English. Maybe he could write it as well. Maybe not.

Raider shook off the ill feeling and kept on for Rock River.

The saloon at Rock River wasn't too crowded, but Raider managed to stir up some curiosity with the offer of free drinks.

It didn't take long to get them into a talk about statehood.

The topic was foremost among the populace. And all of them seemed to be for it.

"This could be a great state!"

"Ain't gonna give nothin' to Montana nor Idaho."

"We need to be in the Union."

More well-wishers crowded in, looking for the free bottle. Raider kept on buying hooch for everyone.

He asked about Dark Hawk and was told that, generally speaking, everybody in the local area had pretty much overlooked the old Indian's mischief, since Dark Hawk was on his way to the new reservation in the north.

Then Raider asked about Half Eagle.

A hush fell over them.

"You heard about Half Eagle?" somebody asked Raider.

The big man nodded. "Ain't heard much."

"Half Eagle's a renegade," one of the barflies replied. "And they say he ain't never gonna settle on the reservation."

"Aw, he will too!"

"The Army'll make him!"

"Yeah, they won't put up with that shit!"

Raider decided that he would rather not meet Half Eagle, unless it was unavoidable.

He steered the conversation back to statehood.

"We ain't gonna let 'em cut up Wyomin'," somebody said.

Raider lifted his glass. "To the great state of Wyomin'."

There was a cheer.

Then somebody was laughing.

Raider looked across the room to see a rough man sitting by himself at a table. He was stocky and wore a gray slicker and a pointed Stetson. He hadn't shaved for a while. He had a hateful laugh.

"Somethin' funny?" Raider asked him.

One of the barflies gaped at Raider. "That's Harley Dixon, stranger. Don't cross him. We ain't got no law in . . ."

Raider waved the man off. "I want to hear what Mr. Harley Dixon has to say. Go on, Harley."

The man frowned at him. "This godforsaken terr'tory ain't never gonna be a state. Too many idiots around here. Like you." He pointed right at Raider.

The barflies backed away from him.

Raider squared his shoulders, still smiling at the man. "Ain't no need to be mean about it."

"Nothin' but rock and mountains and cold, Wyomin'. I ain't never seen worse country in my life."

Raider wasn't taking his tirade personally, but he did have an instant aversion to the man's arrogant matter.

Dixon started to stand up.

Raider dropped his hand beside his Peacemaker.

Dixon froze in the wooden chair.

The bar crowd scattered in a hurry.

Raider watched the man's hands. "It's a bad day for dyin', Harley."

His hands were on the table.

Smart, Raider thought. No mistake about it. Harley didn't want to draw. But he didn't want to back off either.

"What's it gonna be, Harley?"

The man pointed a finger at him. "I'll see you again."

Raider nodded toward the door. "Get the hell out of here."

Harley got up and crashed through the swinging doors.

Raider turned back to the bar and poured himself a drink.

Then he spun again, just to make sure that Harley wasn't coming back.

Nobody burst through the doors.

Raider relaxed, throwing back a shot of the red-eye.

Gradually his supporters returned to his side, but he was already sick of them, so he left the saloon, striding back toward his horse.

It was dark, hard to see the man who rushed at him from the shadows, his hand holding a big knife that fell straight for Raider's chest.

"Mr. Wagner?"

Wagner looked up from his desk to see the telegraph operator standing before him. "Yes?"

The man thrust a piece of paper at him. "This came from Raider. I thought I'd bring it myself."

Wagner read the terse message and sighed.

"Is he all right?" the key operator asked.

Wagner nodded as he read the message a second time.

"You know," the telegraph man said, his head turning in

wonder, "I always wondered what it would be like to be a Pinkerton. Travelin' all over. Lots of action."

"Yes," Wagner replied, "but the job has its drawbacks as well."

The man just nodded and turned away, heading for the door.

Drawbacks, Wagner thought. Like big, irresponsible Arkansas natives who sent three-sentence messages. Raider had barely finished one case and now he was already involved in another.

"Just a minute," Wagner called to the key operator. "I have to give you the number for Raider's back pay."

"Yes, sir."

Wagner looked in his book. "Thirty-eight dollars, less four dollars for both telegrams. Thirty-four dollars."

"Send it to Laramie?"

Wagner said that would be fine.

When the telegraph operator left, Wagner tried to concentrate on his work, but he found himself thinking about Raider over and over again.

Harley Dixon came out of the shadows with the knife and lunged at Raider, but the big man was quicker.

Raider dipped a shoulder and grabbed Harley's arm, swinging the husky bushwhacker into the hitching post.

Harley grunted, grabbing his back.

Raider lifted his boot and planted a hard kick in the man's leathery gut. Harley grunted again, sinking to one knee. Raider laced a second kick to Harley's face. That put the greasy ambusher in the dirt.

Harley tried to get up.

Raider stepped on his knife hand and then drew his Colt.

He pressed the barrel of the Peacemaker to Harley's ear. "I oughta kill you right now, you tub of guts."

"No," the fallen man groaned.

They always wanted mercy after you kicked their asses.

Raider figured it wouldn't be right to shoot him. So he kicked him again in the gut. Harley coughed up some blood.

"Don't cross me again, Dixon, or I'll have to kill you the next time."

Harley made a low, hateful noise.

Raider moved around to the other side of the roan. He untied the reins and swung into the saddle. He wanted to get back to Walters's place, to talk to the rancher.

He wondered if Becky would be mad at him when he got there.

Raider arrived late at the Double-W. A light still burned in Walters's room. He stabled the roan and headed back to the lodge.

Big Bill met him in the main parlor. "Heard you ride up, Raider."

He nodded at the rancher. "How 'bout we have a snort and talk some?"

Walters studied the big Pinkerton's face. "You got bad news?"

Raider sighed. "Well, not really. At least I don't think so."

Big Bill went to get the bottle. When he came back, he poured them glasses of Irish whiskey and then threw another log on the fire. "Well," he said finally, "let's have it."

Raider knocked back the whiskey. "As far as I can see, you ain't got a hell of a lot to worry about, Big Bill."

He told the rancher about the mostly favorable reaction he had found to the notion of statehood.

His mention of Harley Dixon brought a frown to Big Bill's face. He had heard of the ne'er-do-well, that he was one of the few who had been talking down statehood, and said that he should have told Raider about him in the first place. Raider agreed, but said there was no harm done.

"I found out who's been rustlin' your cows," Raider offered.

Walters seemed astonished. "That didn't take long."

Raider shrugged. "I got lucky. Ran into a Crow Indian name of Dark Hawk. He's been takin' a few cows from your herd."

Walters nodded. "I suspected as much."

"He said he's goin' north, back to the reservation."

"Yes," the rancher rejoined, "that's the gossip. I'm more worried about his son, Half Eagle."

"Dark Hawk said to tell you that Half Eagle ain't goin' north," Raider offered. "He seemed to think that information might be worth a few cows."

"It is. Now I know who to watch for."

Raider scowled at the rancher. "Look here, Walters, if you knew all this already, why'd you bring me in?"

Walters exhaled and stood up. "All right, I had my suspicions. But your good work has proven out what I've thought all along. The truth is, I have something else in mind, Raider, and I want you to help me."

Raider frowned. "Go on, my ears are workin'."

Walters seemed to fill with energy. "I want to have a meeting," he said, gesturing to the sky. "A big wingding. Invite everyone in the territory. Slaughter some steers. Have a barbecue. Invite the powers that be in the territory. Have a public meeting. Rally the cause of statehood."

Raider chortled a little. "Hell, that sounds good to me, Big Bill. But why do you need me here?"

"To make sure nothing gets out of hand," Walters replied. "You're a Pinkerton. You're tough and good with a gun. I'll invite the marshal, too, and some of the officers from Fort Laramie. Hell, anyone can come. A big meeting for everyone. I'm gonna call it a statehood caucus."

Raider figured there was no reason why he couldn't stay and do a few days of easy duty.

There was one thing still bothering him. "Walters, didn't you say somebody wrote 'Get Out Now' in blood next to one of them dead cows?"

The rancher nodded. "Why?"

"Just seems strange," Raider said. "I got to wonder if those Injuns could write like that."

Walters waved him off. "Probably Half Eagle. They say he went to a white school for a while."

"He got anythin' agin' you?" Raider asked.

"No, not personal. I let his father steal my cows. I look the other way like a lot of people around here."

The big man glanced sideways at Walters. "Anythin' else you know that you ain't tellin' me, Big Bill?"

Walters tried to look penitent. "Raider, I know I threw you out there pretty quick. But you did sign on."

"What you didn't tell me coulda got me killed," he warned. "No more s'prises, Big Bill. *Comprende?*"

"Just stay on for the big party," Walters replied. "I'll make it up to you, Raider. I promise."

Raider figured that would do for the moment. After all, there hadn't been any real damage. Not yet, anyway. That would all come later, like the breaking dam that was never expected, the flash flood in the middle of the night.

Raider yawned, still unaware of his future troubles. "Reckon I'll get some shut-eye."

"I'm gonna do that myself," Walters replied.

The big man went up to the loft and settled into bed in a hurry.

He was almost asleep when Becky slid in beside him.

She put her lips close to his ear. "I thought you'd never get back."

Her hand gripped him.

He rolled over to protest, but instead found himself kissing her.

Becky parted her legs.

Raider slipped inside her, making her groan with a low, woeful whisper of pleasant excitement.

CHAPTER NINE

After two weeks of easy duty at the Double-W, Raider was beginning to feel a little guilty.

He had done some work in helping Walters prepare for the statehood caucus, to be held on the grounds of the ranch. Raider had ridden to various settlements to post notices and sound out the populace as to their views on statehood—almost all of them were for Wyoming joining the Union. A few naysayers spoke up, but they were always shouted down.

Raider couldn't spur them either way, as he figured to do so was to campaign, and that was against the rules of the Pinkerton Agency. He figured it was bending the rules for him to put up the posters, but he did it anyway, mainly because they simply called people to the meeting, nothing more. If the posters had spoken to either side of the statehood cause, he wouldn't have done it, not even for Walters.

And Raider had to admit that he liked Big Bill. The rancher was a good host and drinking companion. After one of Becky's fine dinners—she spent most of her time in the kitchen now—the big Pinkerton and the rancher would retire to the comfort of the hearth and the bottle, sipping fine whiskey, talking about anything that popped into their heads.

Walters asked Raider a lot of questions, which were answered despite Raider's usual reluctance to become familiar with anyone.

"How come you like to carry the Peacemaker when there are a lot more guns around these days?"

"The .45 just feels good in my hand, Big Bill. The rest of them peashooters are like toy popguns."

"How come you ain't never married, Raider?"

"Well, I ain't the kind for listenin' to it from women. My old partner, Doc Weatherbee, got married, but I reckon it ain't for me, Big Bill."

"What about Becky?"

"You're the one with the ranch, Walters. Why don't you offer her a job as your housekeeper?"

"I already have, big man. She says she's gonna stay with you."

"Not for all the cows in Texas, Montana, and Wyomin'!"

And so it went. Lazy days waiting for the big rally and lazy nights with good food, whiskey, and Becky next to him. Easy duty. He just hoped he didn't have to pay for it somewhere down the road.

Raider had always felt a sense of balance about his work and the world around him. The world presented most of its troubles to idle hands. Raider always got in a stew when he took too much time to himself. Like the time in El Paso when a vacation had landed him in a cell next to a kid named William Bonney—Billy the Kid.

Still, his stay at the Double-W had been so pleasant that he hadn't made any effort to get out of the duty, even if it did make him feel something of an idler. He kept Wagner at bay with telegrams twice weekly, saying that he was offering protection to William Walters, that he would continue until Big Bill didn't need him anymore. What the hell did Wagner care, as long as the fee was paid promptly to the agency.

Becky would be a problem when it finally came time to leave her. But Raider couldn't be cold to her. Life at the ranch seemed to agree with Becky, too. She had filled out some, her skin had taken on a healthier tone, and her cheeks were rosy but not from rouge. She looked like an innocent farm girl.

Two weeks of paradise. Even the weather held pretty good, except for an occasional burst of rain. The air was cooler, chilled by autumn, but fine for riding and hunting.

Two weeks with Becky.

The big rally was only a week away.

Raider figured he could stand it that long.

Allan Pinkerton's return to the agency sparked a certain amount of tension in his employees.

The boss immediately called Wagner into his office for a status report.

Wagner assured him that the cases were going fine. "Even Raider," he told the commander. "He's reporting in twice a week by wire from Laramie. I believe he's finally adhering to procedure."

Pinkerton frowned. "Raider following procedure. That *is* rare. Where the devil is he anyway?"

"Wyoming," Wagner replied. "He's working for a rancher as a personal bodyguard. It doesn't seem like much, but the rancher doesn't mind paying our fees. He seems to be quite well off."

Pinkerton stared straight at his second-in-command. "The rancher's name wouldn't be Walters, would it?"

Wagner gaped at his superior. "Why, yes, how did you know?"

Pinkerton made a funny noise in the back of his throat. "Hah. Walters's name is all over the place. You forget, I was down in Nebraska, near the Wyoming territorial border. All the talk is of statehood. There's even supposed to be some sort of rally at Walters's ranch."

Wagner frowned. "Sounds terribly political. Do you think Raider's smart enough to stay out of the political side?"

"He knows the rules, William, though he's not one to go by the book very much. Still, I don't think he'd be involved if he was doing something that goes against the bylaws of this agency."

Wagner sighed. "Well, I can pull him off the case if you want me to. It doesn't seem logical to use a man with Raider's talents for a simple bodyguard case. We could put one of our new men on it."

Pinkerton shook his head. "No, let him stay. If he's not finished in another week, we'll call him in."

Wagner agreed that was the thing to do.

"Anything else?" Pinkerton asked.

Wagner shrugged. "Well . . . there are a few things that only you can clear up, but it's mostly papers that require your signature. They're all on your desk so you can attend to them at your leisure."

Pinkerton looked down at his desk, the signal for Wagner to leave.

Wagner returned to his desk, sinking into his chair. He knew he shouldn't feel worried about Raider, especially since the big galoot was on easy duty. Still, the big man from Arkansas had neglected to tell Wagner about the rally at Walters's ranch. Something like that could cause lots of complications for an agent. He just hoped Raider knew what he was doing.

The week before the statehood caucus had been unsettling, especially when the telegram had come from Laramie. It was for Raider, sent by Wagner to warn him not to get involved in any political schemes. Raider had to wonder how Wagner had heard about the caucus. He hadn't figured on word traveling all the way back to Chicago. Still, there it was, in black and white.

Raider stood on the front porch of Walters's lodge, reading the message.

The rancher came out of the house and stood next to him. "Trouble?"

Raider shook his head, even though he could not really see the message as a good omen. "Nothin' to worry about."

Walters clapped him on the shoulder. "Come on. I want to show you somethin'. Ever'thing's almost finished."

Raider looked out on the confusion that had reigned over the Double-W for the last six days. Walters had hired extra men to slaughter the steers and build the huge fires for the barbecue. Water barrels and troughs had been set out to accommodate settlers and their animals. Signs were erected to direct campers to designated areas for their overnight stay. The rally was slated for the last Saturday and Sunday in October, which was cause for concern. Walters was afraid it might snow before everyone got there.

As they walked among the workers, Walters shook his head. "If I hadn't wanted to get right to this, I could have held it in the summer."

Raider gazed toward the horizon. "Well, free grub has a way of drawin' people out. And let's face it, Big Bill, there ain't a hell of a lot to do in Wyomin'. Sodbusters, miners, farmers, cow men—they're all gonna come 'cause nobody ever invited 'em to nothin' before in their whole life."

Walters looked up at the banner that was being erected between two poles. It read, "Welcome Wyomingers." The letters in each word had to be five feet high.

"I hope you're right, Raider. I sure do."

The big Pinkerton pointed toward the horizon. "Look, there's dust there. Somebody already on the way to the picnic."

They both watched as the rider came in from the south. It wasn't a guest of the caucus. It was one of Walters's men.

The rider reined up before he reached the festivities.

Raider and Big Bill went to meet him.

"Trouble?" Walters asked.

The man shrugged. "I ain't sure. We found another dead steer. It was killed with this."

He took something from inside his shirt. It was a broken arrow. A Crow arrow. Raider immediately recognized the markings.

"Dark Hawk," he said.

Walters frowned and sighed. "You sure?"

"It's either him or Half Eagle," the rider offered.

Walters looked at Raider. "What do you think, big 'un?"

Raider had a serious expression on his rugged face. "I think I better go have a look. This ain't the kind of thing you want to get started the day before your meetin'."

The rancher agreed. "Take my stallion if you want. And get this man a fresh horse."

Raider strode toward the stable. He knew things had been too quiet. Too much easy duty. And now this dead steer had turned up the day before everyone was supposed to arrive for the big meeting.

Maybe it wasn't anything to worry about. Just Injun mischief. Maybe it was the tail-end of Half Eagle's rustling.

He tried not to think it, but it came into his head. Maybe it was the beginning of something else.

Raider decided to ride Big Bill's stallion. The animal was faster than any other mount in the stable. And by now everyone knew there was a Pinkerton at the ranch. Word had gotten around, so no one would question the fact that Raider was on Walters's horse.

The rider who had brought the news chose a fresh horse and went with him.

They drove hard to the south on the rolling plain. It took them the better part of an hour to find the dead steer. There was a surprise waiting for them beside the animal.

Written in the dirt and soaked with the steer's blood were the words "You had your chance."

The rider turned pale. "That wasn't there when I found this steer."

Raider tipped back his Stetson. "You sure?"

"I never saw it, pardner. And I can tell you, I wouldn't have missed somethin' like that. I can read."

Was somebody really trying to send Walters a message?

Or was if Half Eagle playing games?

Raider tried to figure reasons to be worried, but he finally decided that one renegade couldn't do much against the whole territory, which was about to ride down on the Double-W for the big to-do.

Still, it might be worth a look around.

Raider turned in a circle, surveying the area.

"Whatcha lookin' for?" the rider asked.

"The man who did this has to have a place to hide," Raider offered. "Now, if he wrote that in the dirt after you found the steer, he was close by when you found it."

"Sounds right to me."

Raider saw the mountains in the distance. That was where the rustler had gone. He could hide anywhere for a little while. Crouch low. Watch the man discover the dead steer, come back, and scratch the warning in the dirt.

"He's prob'ly out there watchin' us," the rider said.

Raider told the man to go back to the ranch. "Tell Walters to get his hands mobilized. Maybe get the herd in a good safe place."

"What're you gonna do?"

"Have a look in those hills," Raider replied as he swung into the saddle.

The other man rode off, heading back toward the Double-W.

Raider made for the rise in the distance. He figured it would be hard to find the renegade in his own territory. Half Eagle probably knew every inch of the plain and the mountains. But even if Raider couldn't find him, he still wanted the renegade to know there was somebody on his trail.

Raider was ready to give up his search when he saw the man's shape high up against the clear sky. A lone man. The form hesitated for a moment before it disappeared behind a rock. Was it Half Eagle?

Maybe that was how the renegade had gotten his name. Could he fly like the bird that soared on the wind currents? Raider quickly dismounted and stood behind the black, watching the shadows of the mountain.

He drew the rifle from the scabbard. It wasn't his own '76, but the '73 Winchester that Walters kept on his saddle. Raider figured it didn't matter. The dark shape was too high for any kind of shot.

Still, he squeezed off a round in the air to see if there would be any reply. What if Half Eagle had a band of men in the hills? They might ride down on Raider and make it a real fight.

"Half Eagle!"

The echo of his voice rolled through the air.

Nothing from high up.

"You can't get away with it forever, Half Eagle. Somebody's gonna come after you!"

The shadow appeared above him again, silhouetted against the sky. For a moment, Raider thought he heard laughter. But then the shape disappeared again, bobbing back into the rocks.

Raider studied the slopes, wondering if he could get up there.

What would he do if he got near the renegade?

Shoot him?

It would more likely be the other way around. Half Eagle was at home on the mountain. What if the Indian was the one who got off the lucky shot?

Raider knew better than to chase the renegade, even if it did hurt his pride to know that he was backing away from a challenge.

He also couldn't shake the feeling that sooner or later he was going to have to face Half Eagle.

But for now there was no harm done. Just the dead steer and the cocky renegade. And he couldn't see how either one was a threat to the big statehood caucus.

So he climbed into the saddle of the black, gazing toward the mountains one more time. "Give it up, Half Eagle!"

The echo rose and died in a few seconds.

Something thudded in the dirt at the feet of the stallion.

Raider recognized the same kind of Crow arrow that had killed the steer.

He glared toward the shadows in the rocks. "I'll see you later, Half Eagle. You can count on that."

He spurred the black, heading back toward the Double-W, never thinking that he would find more trouble when he returned.

As Raider drew closer to the lodge, he saw that a buggy had been parked in front of the porch. Several of Big Bill's hired hands were standing on the porch talking. They all turned toward Raider as he rode up on the black stallion.

He came out of the saddle, frowning at the buggy. "What's this all about?" he asked them.

Before they could answer, Becky rushed from the house and wrapped her arms around the big man's waist. This brought hidden smiles and subdued laughter from the hired hands. They didn't want the Pinkerton to get mad at them, but they still thought the woman's attentions were a worthy form of amusement. They were just jealous that Raider had a woman.

"What is it, honey?"

Becky had been crying. "It's horrible," she replied, looking up at him. "There's this awful man who came to see Big Bill. They're fightin' in his study. I heard them shouting."

Raider patted her shoulder. "Don't worry, Becky. I'll have a look."

She drew back a little. "I don't want nobody to hurt Big Bill."

Raider glanced toward the other hands. "What y'all know 'bout this?"

They all shrugged and said they weren't sure who had come to visit their boss. Maybe it had something to do with the big wingding. They had never seen the man before.

He told them to keep an eye on Becky. When they grinned, he told them not to bother her, just to make sure she didn't come into the house until the business inside was finished.

With that, he opened the front door and went into the lodge.

He hesitated, listening. Nothing at first. Then their voices rose up, resounding through the house.

Raider moved quickly toward Big Bill's room. He figured the rancher had enough weapons to take care of himself, but he still wanted to be nearby. When he was closer, he stopped by the door. He could finally make out what they were saying.

"I don't see why you have to do this, Walters. It's really not necessary. Why can't you leave well enough alone?"

Big Bill's voice came through the closed door. "Because I'm afraid that men like you are gonna scoop up this territory and throw it away like it was gravel in a gold miner's pan."

"But a meeting? Do you know what kind of riffraff you're going to drag in from the plain and the mountains?"

"That riffraff happens to be the same men and women who settled this territory, Blaylock. Now, if you don't mind, I have business to take care of. My guests will be coming soon, and there's no way that I could stop them even if I wanted to."

"I can make it worth your while."

"Good day, Mr. Blaylock!"

There was a deadly quiet.

Then the door swung open and Raider was looking at a slim man with an angular face. He wasn't too young or too old. But he was angry, fuming. His eyes were wide.

"Excuse me!" he said to Raider.

The big man stepped out of his way.

The man started for the front door, but turned before he got there. "See if you can talk some sense into him!" the man cried.

He departed, taking the buggy south. Raider went to the window and watched him go. The buggy wheels stirred dust in the afternoon air.

Big Bill Walters came up beside Raider. "That varmint. I bet we haven't seen the last of him."

Raider's eyes narrowed as he turned to face the rancher. "I thought we agreed there wouldn't be no more surprises, Walters."

A sigh from the burly gent. "I hadn't counted on Blaylock. I thought he'd leave us alone."

"Blaylock?"

"He's the leader against statehood. Figures the territory will be better divided up and given away. I never have been able to find out why Blaylock doesn't want Wyomin' to join the Union. And he won't tell me. Just keeps sayin' that I shouldn't have this caucus."

Raider turned away from the window. "What's his full name?"

"Artis. Artis Blaylock."

"He from around here?"

Walters shrugged. "I ain't sure. He's been around for a couple of months. Stays in Cheyenne. I reckon that's why it took him so long to get out here. But I got a feelin' he ain't gonna go away."

Becky came back in, running straight to Raider. "Oh, that awful man is gone. I'm so glad."

Raider patted her shoulder. "Honey, me and Big Bill are hungry. You think you could go fix us somethin'?"

She gazed up at him, smiling. "Anything for my man."

When she was gone, Big Bill shook his head. "I wish that girl liked me the way she likes you."

Raider urged the rancher toward the hearth. "That ain't nothin' to worry about, Big Bill. We got other lookouts."

The rancher frowned. "What are you talkin' about?"

"Break open the hooch and I'll tell you."

• • •

Walters shook his head back and forth, frowning, staring into the fire. They had been drinking from the bottle of brandy. Raider wasn't sure which was warmer, the fireplace or his guts.

"This is the wrong damned time for Half Eagle to start up. Hell, we just got rid of his daddy. Now he wants to ride wild asses all over the damned countryside."

Raider exhaled dejectedly. "Well, I ain't sure we got to worry about Half Eagle so much as that man who was here before, Blaylock."

Walters turned toward Raider. "Why do you think that?"

"Half Eagle is gonna stay hidden if he sees a bunch of white men comin' to your spread. He ain't gonna want to tangle with a whole lot of palefaces. Might get the Army out after him."

The rancher was doubtful. "If he don't want to cause trouble, then why's he killin' my steers?"

"Oh, he wants to cause trouble all right. But not for himself. Besides, if Half Eagle does show his face, we got enough men to handle him."

"Are you sayin' that Blaylock can cause more trouble than that renegade?" Big Bill asked.

Raider stared into the fire, pondering. "Well, he's just like Half Eagle. Came out of nowhere. And he's agin' you for a real reason, not just causin' trouble 'cause he's got his back up. And if he's agin' you, that means there's somethin' in it for him or for somebody."

Walters stood up, pacing back and forth. "What if nobody comes for my caucus? What if I'm here all by myself?"

Raider didn't get a chance to reply.

Becky came in to announce supper.

"We'll talk about it later," the big man urged.

Walters picked up the brandy bottle and took it with him to the dinner table. "Why did all this have to happen now?" he said as he sat down.

Raider felt sort of good about the sudden turn of events. At least there was a chance he could earn some of his pay now. With the renegade on the loose and the sudden entrance of Artis Blaylock, it gave him something to worry about. For a while, anyway, it seemed as though the easy duty was over.

"Now y'all dig in," Becky said, placing a loaf of fresh-baked bread in front of Raider.

The big man ate heartily, but Big Bill only had an appetite for brandy.

"Don't worry," the girl said in a sweet voice. "Ever'thing will be all right, Daddy."

She patted Big Bill on the shoulder. He touched her hand. Becky smiled and kissed him on the cheek.

Raider was just finishing dinner when the commotion arose outside.

Somebody knocked on the front door. "Mr. Walters, come quick."

Raider reached for his Colt. "What now?"

They rushed through the lodge, emerging onto the front porch.

One of Walters's hired hands pointed to the south. "We just spotted 'em, Mr. Walters. There seems to be a bunch of 'em on the way."

Big Bill frowned. "Can it be?"

Raider clapped him on the shoulder. "And you were worried that nobody'd show up. Hell, there must be a hundred of 'em, and they're all a day early."

They all peered toward the throng of travelers who were making their way toward the Double-W. Takers for Big Bill's free food and hospitality. Moving forward like ants on their way home to the hill. Comin' for the big statehood caucus.

Big Bill grinned. "Well, I'll be. I reckon I oughta go out to meet them. Get 'em settled before dark."

Raider said that was the right thing to do, that he'd go with Big Bill to meet the travelers. But Raider wasn't smiling, even though the caucus now appeared to be under way. The big man from Arkansas figured his job was just beginning.

CHAPTER TEN

The sun was high overhead, making the crisp October day a bright one. A cool breeze blew over the plain, but it was still tolerable weather for the Wyoming territory. Big Bill's guests seemed to be enjoying the vibrant Saturday afternoon, no doubt getting ready for the big feast that evening. They were all anticipating the barbecue that would soon be roasting over the giant fires laid by the extra hands. Big Bill had also seen to it that kegs of beer had been brought from Laramie. No need to let his guests go dry. Besides, the beer would make them loose, eager to hear what Big Bill had to say about statehood.

Raider rode among the travelers, counting them, wondering what would happen if the thousand-odd citizens of the territory decided to make trouble. He wasn't all that excited about a thousand boondogglers drinking beer and getting liquored up. A thousand, that was when he had stopped counting. The numbers seemed to be growing all day.

By late afternoon, the plain was covered with tents and wagons almost as far as the eye could see from horseback. They were still setting up camp, digging latrines, pitching tents, making fires. Men, women, children, babies—most of them dirt poor. Were these really the people to whom Big Bill wanted to carry his message, the holy word of statehood?

"Hey, you, cowboy? What time do we eat?"

Raider glanced down at the weather-beaten sodbuster who stood next to his wife and two kids. "Won't be long," the big man replied.

He urged the horse away from their expectant faces, starting a wide circle around the camp.

At first glance, everything seemed calm enough. But there were still plenty of rough-looking men among the guests—men who had arrived with one burro, a six-gun, and the clothes on their backs. What the hell would Raider do if a bunch of them started trouble? He couldn't start shooting, not with all the innocent women and children in the crowd.

He kept circling, making his way back to the lodge.

More citizens rolling up from the south, coming down from the north. How far had word reached in the territory? And what about those who were against statehood? Would they come to have their say?

He rode up to the lodge and dismounted.

Walters was standing on the porch, beaming at the success of his endeavor. "Hello, Raider. You been out amongst 'em?"

The big man frowned and nodded. "Yeah, I have."

Walters brow fretted. "Raider, you seem sad. What seems to be the trouble, friend?"

Raider tied the reins of his mount to the hitching post. "You got more'n a thousand of 'em out there, Walters. I know, I counted."

Walters let out a complacent sigh. "It couldn't have worked out better, Raider. They'll carry the word back to where they came from."

"Maybe. I just hope nobody decides to make a ruckus. I'd hate to have to shoot into a crowd."

Walters laughed, shaking his head. "I don't think you'll have to do that, Raider. Hard for a man to be riled with a full belly and a glass of beer."

"I hope you're right, Big Bill."

They sat on the porch, watching as the barbecue pits began to smoke. Walters had even brought in a few pigs to roast. He had to lock up his own smokehouse. He didn't want any of the guests to raid his personal cache of smoked meat.

"They're hungry," Raider offered. "Better start feedin' 'em."

Walters nodded. "I suppose you're right."

Walters waved to one of his men and the dinner bell began to ring.

A cheer went up through the wave of campers.

"No turnin' back now," Walters offered.

Raider just nodded, watching as the guests began to line up for their free meal. They seemed to be calm enough. Honest, well-mannered folk, despite their poverty. He wondered if they would stay that way after they had several snoutfuls of free beer.

Becky came out onto the porch, frowning at the throng. She felt sort of pushed aside, since she didn't have anyone to cook for. Standing next to Raider, she put her hand on his shoulder. "Look at all of them," she said sadly. "They can't wait to sink their teeth into that free food."

Raider patted her hand. "Aw, don't worry, honey. You'll have your ranch back soon as they're gone."

She moved around and sat on his lap. "Where's Big Bill?"

"He went out to talk to some of 'em," the big man replied.

Becky pouted a little. "Didn't even ask me if I wanted to help with the cookin'."

"There's more'n a thousand of 'em out there, Becky. Big Bill didn't want you to be right in the middle of 'em."

She turned back to Raider, smiling. "Well, since we ain't got nothin' else to do, want to go upstairs and..."

He urged her off his lap. "Ain't got time for that, Becky. Not now. Big Bill needs me to keep a' eye on things."

Becky protested, at least until Raider told her to be quiet.

His eyes were trained toward the south, peering at the dust that rose on the plain. A rider. Coming headlong for the gathering.

He pointed toward the dust. "Look there, Becky. Somebody comin' strong. I hope it ain't trouble."

Becky folded her arms. "Who could it be?"

"Maybe just another freeloader. Maybe somebody else."

Raider immediately thought of the man who was opposed

to Big Bill's notions of statehood. What was his name? Blaylock?

The rider kept coming hard toward the lodge. His mount circled the crowd, many of whom took notice of his arrival. Raider stood up and checked his Colt. Then he told Becky to go inside.

"I ain't gonna," she replied. "I'm gonna stay right here beside you."

He shook his head, exhaling. "Suit yourself, honey. But don't blame me if the shootin' starts."

Becky turned pale, but she still stayed on the porch.

The rider came to a dusty halt in front of the lodge. He climbed down and immediately asked for water. Said he had come all the way from Cheyenne. That he was as dry as a desert rat.

When he had drank a dipper full of water, the man looked at Raider. "Are you William Walters?"

Raider shook his head. "Nope, but if you tell me what you want with him, I might be able to find him."

The man reached into his saddlebag and pulled out an envelope. "I brung this from Cheyenne. For Walters."

Raider tipped back his Stetson and then pointed toward the crowd. "He's out there, hombre. Why don't you go have a look? Free beef and beer."

"That sounds like it might be worth the walk," the man replied. "Can I tie my horse here?"

"Sure."

Raider let the messenger get a head start and then followed him toward the gathering. The man made his way between the hungry guests, asking for Walters. Finally he came face to face with Big Bill.

Raider hesitated, keeping his hand on his Colt. But the man didn't bother Walters. He only handed him the dispatch from Cheyenne.

Walters opened the letter and read it quickly. He was smiling when he looked up again. He saw Raider standing there. "Where'd you come from, big 'un?"

Raider nodded toward the messenger, who was now in line for his free meal. "Keepin' watch on that one brung you a letter."

Walters waved the dispatch in the air. "Well, it's good and bad news. From the territorial governor. Says he can't make it, but he also says he's behind statehood one hundred percent."

"Congratulations, Big Bill."

Walters grinned like a possum stealing peaches. "Wait till I tell 'em that at the big rally tonight."

"Gonna be speechifyin'?" Raider asked.

"All that I can, big 'un. All that I can."

Raider was sorry to hear that. He always hated listening to political speeches. But he had no choice. He still had to keep an eye on things. Something didn't feel right. And he wasn't quite sure what it was, until he saw the black buggy making tracks for the lodge, stirring more dust in the cool air of the afternoon.

Raider was back on the front porch again, watching the dust cloud rising. When the black buggy rolled into view, he stuck his head inside the lodge and called for Big Bill, who was practicing his speech. Walters came out to gaze at the approaching wagon.

"Looks like Blaylock's buggy," Raider offered.

"I hope not," Walters replied.

They stood there, watching as the buggy drew closer.

Becky came out to stand with them. "What's wrong now?"

"Nothin'," Big Bill replied. "At least I hope not."

Raider started to tell her to go inside, but he knew she wouldn't do it.

Walters grimaced when the buggy was close enough to see the driver. "Damn, it *is* Blaylock."

"Maybe he just came for a free meal," Becky offered.

Raider sighed. "I doubt that."

"He's got somebody with him," Walters said.

The buggy drew even with the lodge.

Raider gawked at the man who sat next to Artis Blaylock. He had seen the face before. It was cleaner now, close-shaven and washed, but it still belonged to Harley Dixon, the man who had tried to kill him in Rock River.

Walters pointed a finger at Artis Blaylock. "You got no right to be here, Blaylock. Now git off my property."

Raider's hand tickled the handle of his Colt. He was watching

Dixon, who sat there with a dumb expression on his hateful face. Dixon wore a shiny new Remington .44 on his side. It was situated for a cross-draw.

Blaylock smiled at Walters. "Your poster says that anyone can come to your caucus, Big Bill. You don't want to—"

Raider stepped up beside the rancher. "Blaylock, you ain't got no right to come here and bring that troublemaker Dixon."

Harley Dixon glared at Raider like he didn't recognize him.

"What's the matter, Harley?" Raider challenged. "Don't you remember the men you try to kill?"

"I ain't never seen you afore," Dixon said. "I just rode out here for the big barbecue. Somethin' wrong with that?"

Raider pointed a finger at them. "Get gone, Blaylock, Dixon. We don't want no trouble."

"Who says I came to cause trouble?" Blaylock asked in a cool voice.

"Yeah," Dixon echoed, "we didn't come to cause trouble."

Walters had broken a sweat on his forehead. "Blaylock, I mean it. You had better get gone."

Blaylock smiled like a hungry coyote. "Why don't we wait for Bick Johnson? He's on his way out here with his men."

Walters frowned. "The marshal?"

"Yeah," Dixon said. "The marshal."

Blaylock glared at his bodyguard. "That'll be enough, Harley." Then, to Big Bill: "You see, Johnson and his men are hungry. And there's also a group of soldiers on the way. So I wouldn't cause trouble, Bill. Not with all those men on the way."

Raider pointed to Dixon. "What about him?"

"Harley is a hungry man," Blaylock offered. "He just wants to fill his belly. And like the poster says, everybody is welcome. You don't want to go against your word, do you, Walters?"

Big Bill turned sideways, glancing at Raider. "He's got me. I can't very well throw him out, not with the caucus open to everyone. Wouldn't look right to the others."

"Yeah," Raider replied, still glaring at Dixon. "I know. So let 'em stay. I'll keep an eye on 'em. And the marshal is on the way."

Walters scowled at Blaylock. "Go feed your face, Blaylock. But the first time you or that ape gets out of line . . ."

Dixon's face turned red. "Who you callin' a' ape!"

Raider stepped in front of Walters. "Dixon, I'll take you out right now if you don't shut your yap!"

Dixon made a cross-move for his pistol.

Raider came up with the Colt before the bushwhacker could get his hand on the .44.

Dixon gaped at the bore of the Peacemaker.

"Go on," Raider said. "Try it. Be a pity if you and your boss got caught in the cross-fire."

Blaylock snapped at Dixon, telling him to back off. Then he smiled at Walters. "Like I said, Big Bill. We didn't come here to cause trouble. And if your man wants to start something, I can't be responsible for—"

"You're welcome to stay," Walters rejoined. "But if that ape starts a ruckus, I'll see to it that you're both ridden out of here on a rail."

Blaylock tipped his hat. "I think I'll go have myself something to eat, Walters. Good day to you."

He shook the reins of the buggy.

The horse lurched forward, moving away from the porch.

Raider watched as the wagon circled around, heading back toward the encampment of the other guests. "I sure as hell wish he hadn't showed up with Dixon."

He realized that Becky was standing next to him, her body pressed against his. "I'm scared, Raider," she said softly.

He put his arm around her. "Don't be, honey. I'm here. And the marshal will be here soon."

Walters gazed wide-eyed at the big man. "No, don't tell Johnson that Blaylock came here to spite me."

Raider squinted at his associate. "But..."

"No buts," Big Bill replied. "I don't want Johnson to think that there's gonna be any trouble. He might stop the proceedings."

Raider saw his point. "Then I better stay close to Dixon."

"Do that," the rancher replied. "I'm goin' back into the lodge to go over my speech."

"I'll tell some of the other hands," Raider offered. "We'll all keep watch on Dixon and Blaylock."

He started down off the porch.

Becky tried to hang on to him. "What about me?"

"Stay with Big Bill," Raider replied. "Help him with his speech."

"Yes," Walters said. "I could use a hand."

Becky seemed reluctant to leave Raider's side, but she still went inside with the rancher, leaving the tall Pinkerton to stride back toward the crowd where Blaylock and Dixon had disappeared among the guests.

"Hey, watch where you're goin'!"

"Yeah, you can't butt in line!"

"That ain't right."

Harley Dixon turned to glare at several sodbusters. "I can do what I want," he said. "Try and stop me."

Dixon was trying to get ahead of those honest folks who were waiting for a plate of barbecue and a glass of beer.

"He's buttin' in!"

"You ain't s'posed to do that!"

"Somebody stop him!"

Dixon was about to speak again when he felt the hand on his shoulder. He wheeled to look at Raider, whose hand was on the butt of his Peacemaker. Dixon's mouth hung open.

"Thought you wasn't gonna cause trouble," Raider said.

Dixon's eyes narrowed. "Just tryin' to get some grub, Pinkerton."

Murmurs from the crowd.

"Hey, that tall one is a Pink."

"Yeah, I knew that. Heard it all along."

"Pinkerton, huh. Wonder why he's here?"

Raider ignored them, gesturing toward the back of the line. "Why don't you wait your turn like everybody else, Dixon?"

"Yeah, wait your turn!"

"Ain't fair to butt in like that!"

"The Pinkerton's gonna set him straight!"

Dixon looked like he wanted to fight.

Raider had to admit that he was ready. "You remember how I kicked your guts in Rock River, Harley?"

The man's eyes grew wide. "That was you?"

"Shouldn't forget a man you tried to kill, Harley."

The crowd, sensing a fight, had pushed in a little.

Raider and Dixon stood toe to toe, glaring at each other.

Then, before they could exchange blows, the crowd seemed to part and somebody strode toward them. "What seems to be the problem here?"

Marshal Bick Johnson had appeared with several of his deputies behind him.

Raider kept his eyes on Dixon. "This man thinks he's too good to wait in line with the others."

Johnson sized up Dixon. "That true?"

Harley's face went slack, the smiling bully who had done nothing wrong. "Aw, there ain't no trouble, Marshal. I just got mixed up, what with all the people here today. I'll go back."

"Aw hell," said one of the hungry guests, "let him go on through."

"Yeah, he's holdin' up the line."

"I want to eat."

Johnson nodded toward the smoky fire. "Go on, Dixon. But I better not see you causin' more grief."

"Shucks, Marshal, I never meant no harm. I'm hungry just like ever'body else. So I reckon I better eat."

He turned back toward the barbecue.

Johnson looked at Raider. "Come on, I want to talk to you and your boss."

Raider fell in with the marshal, holding his words. He didn't want to complain too much about Dixon, because he didn't want Johnson to stop the rally. They went to the lodge, where they found Big Bill saying his speech for Becky and the bear rugs.

Walters gawked when the marshal entered. "Johnson. Glad to have you here. Did you get somethin' to eat?"

Johnson waved him off. "Just came to make sure there's no trouble, Big Bill. Some of the Army boys are on the way. Don't want nobody gettin' their nose out of joint."

Walters made the sweeping gesture of a grand host. "I promise you, Bick, there ain't gonna be no trouble."

And there wasn't, at least until that night, and then only after Big Bill Walters had finished his speech.

Big Bill was standing on the platform, illuminated by torchlight.

The crowd had gathered in front of him, hanging on every word.

They all stood together, listening to his pleas for statehood. Everybody seemed impressed by the oration, even Marshal Johnson and the soldiers who had come along. Raider was the only one who wasn't staring at Walters. The man from Arkansas kept watching the audience to make sure no one moved against the speaker.

"... so, I say in conclusion. If the territory of Wyomin' is goin' to join the Union, then it's up to every man in this country to work hard. To live a productive, law-abidin' life. We want the kind of citizens that the rest of the Union will be proud of. Citizens like you!"

A cheer, one of many that night, rose over the throng.

"We will not let them take our territory!" Walters cried. "Not as long as every honest man has a breath of life left in him. Honest men like you!"

Another roar. Applause. Sympathetic comments. Prideful words.

Had he not been intent on watching the crowd, Raider would have felt stirred himself.

"Statehood!" Big Bill cried. "That's what we want. Statehood!"

The chant went up, "State-hood, state-hood!"

Walters lifted his arms in a gesture of victory.

That was went Raider saw Artis Blaylock moving toward the platform.

Raider crashed through the spectators, coming face to face with Blaylock. "That's far enough, Artis."

Dixon was right behind his boss. "Out of the way, Pinkerton."

"I'm going to have my say," Blaylock said. "And you can't stop me."

They tried to push past Raider.

The big man stopped him, scuffling with both of them.

Walters was staring down from the platform, worried that the ruckus was going to get out of hand.

Suddenly the marshal was there, trying to stop them.

More scuffling.

Some of the spectators were involved for a moment.

WYOMING AMBUSH 97

Marshal Johnson pulled his gun and fired a shot into the air. "Now, I want everyone to stop it right now."

Blaylock seized the moment. "I thought this was a public meeting, Marshal. And I only want to have my say."

Johnson looked up at Walters, who was still on the platform. "What about it, Big Bill? Are you gonna let this man have his say?"

Raider saw the surrender on Big Bill's face. What else could the rancher do? If he wanted to keep the peace, he had to let Blaylock speak.

Walters nodded. "He's right. It is a public meeting. He can say his piece. Come on, Blaylock. Get it over with."

Raider had no choice but to step aside and let him pass.

Dixon was grinning triumphantly as his boss took the platform. "How you like that, Pinkerton?"

Raider wheeled abruptly and planted a low blow in Dixon's groin. The tub of guts buckled over, groaning. Nobody had seen him throw the punch, not even the marshal. They were all staring at Blaylock, who was starting his speech. So Raider hit him a second time and Dixon fell to the ground.

"What's wrong with him?" somebody asked.

"Too much beer," Raider replied.

He turned with everyone else to watch Blaylock make his speech.

"Friends," the man said, "I know Mr. Walters speaks for statehood. But I'm here to tell you that there's something else that might be better for this godforsaken plain."

The crowd began to grow restless.

"We can break up this territory..."

A few boos and catcalls.

"What's now Wyoming can be part of Idaho, Colorado, and Montana."

"No!"

"That ain't what we want!"

"Statehood! Statehood!"

Walters smiled behind the speaker. The crowd wasn't buying it. But Blaylock tried to go on.

"Yes, you can have statehood! But let Idaho and Colorado and—"

Somebody threw something from the crowd. It whizzed by

Blaylock's ear, barely missing him. Blaylock kept on until another projectile hit him in the chest.

Walters had to step forward, holding up his hands. "Friends, why don't we take a vote? Tell Mr. Blaylock how we really feel! Would that be all right with you, Artis?"

Blaylock glared at the rancher. "I don't see—"

Big Bill ignored him, looking out over the crowd. "All those in favor of statehood, please signify by saying aye."

The echo was almost deafening.

"All those opposed, say nay."

Only the voice of Harley Dixon could be heard raising his protest.

The crowd cheered again.

Walters gestured toward Blaylock. "You're welcome to stay, sir, to enjoy the food and the beer. But I'm afraid these folks aren't interested in what you have to say."

The applause and cheers drove Blaylock off the platform. He turned one last time to scowl at Big Bill Walters. But then he had to go, defeated and shamed, taking Harley Dixon with him.

CHAPTER ELEVEN

Big Bill Walters came down off the platform, moving among his guests, who now seemed more like constituents.

Raider stayed close behind him, watching for signs of Harley Dixon. But there were only well-wishers, clapping Walters on the back, congratulating him for his stand on statehood. It had been an easy crowd to win over, what with their bellies full of beef and beer.

Walters was full of himself. He had faced Blaylock in public and had won—for now. Raider figured Blaylock was the kind to make another try against Big Bill, but it seemed futile in the light of Walters's caucus. Statehood had a good chance if the people pushed hard enough for it.

There was no sign of Blaylock or Dixon. Of course, they wouldn't do anything on a night like this. Too many witnesses. Too much motive if they were caught.

Raider kept on his toes in any case, following the rancher to the huge bonfire that had begun to grow in the center of the encampment.

Even the soldiers stayed on to talk with Big Bill. He even knew one of them from his days in the war. It wasn't long before the soldiers started to sing. Then the campers joined in. Raider knew most of the old songs, but he didn't lift his voice. Instead, he slipped back into the shadows, watching Walters from a hidden point of view.

He came out of the darkness when he saw the marshal on the edge of the crowd. "Johnson!"

The marshal spooked a little. "Darn you, Pinkerton. Why the devil are you hidin' back there anyway?"

"Just doin' my job. Makin' sure Blaylock and that monkey of his don't try nothin'."

Johnson shook his head with admiration. "Did you see the way Walters handled that? He might be governor some day."

Raider eyed the lawman, who was a little tipsy from the free beer. "Johnson, let me hear what you have to say 'bout this statehood."

"Man to man?"

"If you think you can handle it."

Johnson bristled a little. "I wouldn't mind it. This terr'tory needs a rough hand for a while. Some more law might do it good. I think we'd have it if we joined the Union."

"You know anythin' of them who want to break it up?"

Johnson let out an exhausted breath. "Pardner, I got troubles of my own. I'm chasin' two or three outlaws, and now it looks like I might have some trouble with Half Eagle."

"You will," the big man replied.

Johnson gawked at him. "You know somethin'?"

"I saw Half Eagle yesterday. He's hidin' back in the mountains, northwest of here. It ain't far."

"Never get him out of there," the marshal said.

"Nope, not less'n he wants to come out with his hands up."

"He won't do that."

"No, he won't. But he's got the look of a bad renegade, Marshal. You know the kind. Never take to the reservation. Just can't let it rest until they kill somebody. Or get killed."

"Meanness. Pure damned meanness."

Raider turned to look at the bonfire. "You might be mean, too, Johnson, if you was a' Injun. I know I would be."

The marshal let his eyes drift toward the hypnotic flames. "I reckon."

"What do you know 'bout Blaylock?" Raider asked.

"Some say he's from Colorado. Denver."

"And Dixon?"

The marshal shook his head. "Kill him for me and I'll personally give you a reward of a hundred dollars."

"I almost did it in Rock River," the big man offered. "He came at me with a knife."

"Why didn't you?"

Raider looked at him and grinned. "I didn't want to deal with no lawman, Bick. Hell, you start killin' people, even bad ones, and the law's all over you these days."

"By the way, we're even on the horse I gave you. That reward came in from Kansas. I used the rest of the money to have Rogers buried."

Raider squinted at him. "Who?"

"Rogers. Rattler. The outlaw you killed."

"Oh, yeah."

Raider had almost forgotten about the Rattler. "I'm gonna be lookin' into a few things, Johnson. I want to know if I can count on you."

"How's that?" the marshal said.

"I don't know." Raider shrugged. "If somethin' comes up, I'd like you to back me up on the truth."

"I'm a lawful man, Raider. If you find out somebody is breakin' the law, you come tell me. I'll back you up."

"That's all I needed to know, Bick. That's all I needed to know."

The fire had died down.

Most of the campers were on their way back to their tents and wagons.

The soldiers were searching for their mounts.

Marshal Johnson and his deputies had gone home.

And William "Big Bill" Walters was staggering toward Raider with an intoxicated expression of sheer joy.

"I did it," he told the big man. "I really did."

Raider chuckled to himself. "Yeah, Big Bill, you might just be governor someday."

Walters was all lit up. "Do you really think so? Governor. Governor Walters. By golly I like it. By golly I . . ."

He wavered, spiraling toward the ground.

Raider caught him and kept him from falling. "Come on, Big Bill. Let's get you home."

Several of Walters's hands were close by. They offered to take the old boy into the house. Raider let them. He was being paid to guard Walters, not tuck him into bed.

Raider went into the lodge and settled by the fire.

He closed his eyes, waking in a few minutes when Becky touched his face.

She looked so damned pretty in the orange flow from the hearth.

"It's over," she said. "Isn't it?"

Raider pulled her down beside him, wrapping her in his arms. Sometimes it was the best thing in the world to have a sweet woman next to you. It made everything seem a whole lot easier to stomach.

"I heard 'em puttin' Big Bill to bed," Becky told him. "Did he have a good time?"

Raider nodded, smiling a little. "The old dude handled 'em pretty good. Made Blaylock back down."

"I don't like that man," she offered. "He scares me."

Raider kissed her cheek. "I won't let him hurt you."

"Let's go to bed."

She didn't have to ask him twice. He was ready. Even after the long day. *Especially* after the long day. He needed her beside him. She was getting to him. He'd have to draw back sooner or later, but not tonight.

Becky lay back with her white thighs spread.

Raider got on top of her, prodding her immediately.

She was a little dry, but he managed to work it in.

Becky lifted her legs. "Slow. Until I get wet."

He moved it in and out, feeling her give way.

Pretty soon they were bumping against the floor.

"Inside me."

He drove his cock deep, discharging.

Becky cried out as her body trembled.

He lay there with his cock inside her, trying to catch his breath.

Becky pushed him off and closed her eyes. She began to snore. Raider put his head on the pillow and tried to join her.

But sleep didn't come to him. He got up again and put his pants on, heading downstairs to throw another log on the fire.

He sat, leaning back on the skins, staring into the fresh flames that rose up from the embers.

Something didn't feel right.

What the hell was it?

Blaylock. That hateful look on his face when he was defeated at the rally. He had thrown in with Dixon, a man of low character. Blaylock didn't seem like the kind of man who would work for nothing. He had something to gain if he was campaigning against statehood.

Maybe it was all behind them now. Blaylock would accept his loss and live with the consequences. Walters wasn't in any real danger.

Raider realized how much he had come to like and respect the old boy. Walters was tough, strong-minded. The West needed more men like Big Bill. And fewer men like Blaylock.

Came all the way out here to speak against statehood, Raider thought. A long way. Brought his bodyguard the second time. Dixon. The man who had come after Raider with a knife.

What if the thing in Rock River had been planned all along? A ploy to get the Pinkerton who was guarding Walters, the new symbol of statehood. He shook off the chill in his shoulders, deciding that he was thinking too much. This case had been dull for the most part. A few ruffled feathers, but no real harm done.

Big Bill was safe in his bed.

The campers would be leaving in the morning.

Everything had come off right.

No problems.

Raider closed his eyes.

He drifted off, waking the next day to the smell of bacon from Becky's kitchen.

Big Bill was already at the table when Raider came in. The rancher held his face in his hands. A buffalo of a hangover had stampeded him into the dust. He groaned as Raider sat down.

"I never was much of a hard drinker," Walters said.

Raider tried not to smile. "It'll sneak up on you."

Becky set a plate in front of Raider. "How come you went down to sleep by the fire last night?"

Raider shrugged. "I just did."

She turned away, pouting.

Raider dug into his breakfast. She had made eggs over easy with potatoes, onions, and smoked meat. Raider figured he was going to miss her good meals.

Becky put the same thing in front of Walters.

The old gent made a gagging noise and rushed out back to unload.

Raider just reached for the plate, figuring he was lucky to get seconds.

"He might want to eat," Becky said.

"No he don't. He wants to feel better."

Big Bill came in and sat down at the table again. "I ain't never takin' another drink in my life."

"It was that green beer," Raider offered. "Didn't see me drinkin' any of that stuff."

Big Bill moaned, putting his head on the table. "If I felt any worse I'd be dead."

Raider laughed, finishing his second breakfast.

Walters flinched when somebody knocked on the back door. "What the devil do you want?"

One of his hired hands stuck his head into the kitchen. "Mr. Walters, them people want you to say somethin' to 'em before they leave. They're all standin' in front of that platform."

Walters waved the man away. "Tell them I'm sick. Tell 'em I'm dead. I don't care what you tell 'em."

Raider winked at the man. "Give us a few minutes. I'll have him ready to speechify in no time."

Walters gaped sadly at Raider. "What are you talkin' about?"

"Hair of the dog that bit you," the big man replied. "Stay right here, Big Bill. I'll take care of you."

"What should I tell them people?" the hand asked.

"Tell 'em that Walters will be right out."

Raider left the kitchen, making a beeline for Big Bill's liquor cabinet. He came back and slapped a bottle of brandy on the table. Big Bill turned away when Raider popped the cork.

The rancher made a gagging sound. "I can't even stand to smell that consarned demon brew."

Raider tilted the bottle, pouring a generous slug of brandy. "Come on, drink it. It's the only thing that'll make you feel better."

He put the glass in Big Bill's hand. The rancher failed with the first two attempts to lift it to his lips. Raider finally forced him to choke down a whole swallow. A glow seemed to spread over him.

"One more," Raider said. "Go on."

When Walters drained the glass, he stood up from the table. "By golly, I do feel better."

Raider told him to drink some water before he went out to see his guests. His mouth would get dry if he didn't. Best to face his friends with something besides cotton in his mouth.

"And I say to you, people of Wyomin'. Go forth and tell your friends, your family, your neighbors. Anybody you see. Pass the word along. We want statehood. Even if it takes ten years, we will not be denied!"

Big Bill's speech was part sermon and part politics, but it seemed to work on them. They applauded him and cheered his cause. Of course, the remaining sides of beef could have had something to do with their adoration.

"Now y'all help yourselves to anythin' that's left," Walters shouted. "And don't forget to bury your waste!"

They applauded him one more time before he came down from the platform.

He looked at Raider, wiping sweat from his forehead. "I'm glad that's over. Now maybe I can eat some of Becky's cookin'."

Raider urged him toward the house. "Let's go in before they notice you ain't your old self."

When they were back at the lodge, a good meal and another shot of brandy restored Big Bill's spirit. "By golly, I think we earned some converts. I'm glad I sent 'em home happy."

"Yeah," Raider rejoined, "they'll be loyal to you till somebody else feeds 'em and gives 'em a shot of beer."

Walters peered at the big man from Arkansas. "Raider, I got to thank you for helpin' me. I'm sure gonna miss you."

Raider figured it was time to talk business. "Yep, I reckon it's time for me to move on, Big Bill. I'd watch out for that Blaylock and his goon. But I think you'll be all right."

The rancher frowned, looking at his brandy glass. "Becky is gonna take it pretty hard when you leave, Raider."

"Well, we don't have to tell her I'm goin'. And when she finds out I'm gone, you can give her your shoulder to cry on. She might even marry you if you play it right. Hell, where else has she got to go?"

Walters was bolstered by the hope of having Becky for his wife. "Raider, how about you and me doin' a little huntin' before you go? I think I can put us onto some elk. One of my hands claims to have spotted a herd not far from here. Feel like tryin' it?"

Raider knew he should say no. But the rancher's hospitality was too much, in the final bargain. Just another day or two. What could it hurt?"

That night, after they had shaken the floor of the loft, Becky slid close to Raider, putting her mouth against his ear. "What time will y'all be back from huntin'?"

Raider knew that he planned to leave straight from the trip, not to come back at all. "I ain't sure."

"You think Big Bill will keep you on for a while?"

He didn't want to lie, but it was the easiest way. "Yeah, I should be around here for another two or three weeks."

"Where will *we* go after that?"

Her words cut right through him. "Oh, I don't know. Where would you like to go, Becky?"

"New Orleans! I just know I'd love it there. You can get a job and I'll find a house for us."

"Sure. Now let's get some sleep. I got to get up early if me and Big Bill are gonna get them elk."

"New Orleans! I know I'm gonna love it."

Raider wondered if he had made a mistake by staying the extra day.

He hated breaking her heart, but he figured she was tough enough to recover in a hurry. And Big Bill wanted her to stay with him. He was doing the right thing. Maybe it didn't feel good to him, but he knew it was for the best.

He'd really feel like a fool when he turned out to be wrong.

They rode out before daybreak, heading north.

One of Walters's hired hands was guiding them. He had seen a herd of elk north of the ranch. He thought he could find them again.

The sun was just peeking over the horizon when they found the tracks in the soft earth.

Raider watched as Big Bill went into action. He was a good tracker. He took the lead after that, following the herd.

"Some big bucks in this one," he told Raider, "but I don't know if we'll find 'em in time. They may be out of reach 'fore long."

"I don't know, Mr. Walters," the hired hand offered. "They probably just come down from the high country. It's that time of year. They'll be here until the snow's all come and gone."

"You got a point," Walters replied. "But if they're back in those trees north of here, we won't be able to chase 'em."

Raider wondered if the rancher wanted to beg off. "I don't care much about huntin', Big Bill. If you want to..."

Walters shook his head. A gleam had come into his eyes. He was a man who didn't enjoy failure of any kind.

"Let's press on. We'll find 'em soon enough."

They mounted up and rode again, until Big Bill found more tracks. The herd had turned west a little, heading for high ground. That was better, he told Raider. They might be able to catch them in a narrow corner.

"I'd like for you to get a shot with your '76," Walters told the big man from Arkansas.

Raider said it didn't matter much to him. "One thing, Big Bill. We're in Half Eagle country. He might be out there watchin' us."

Walters laughed. "Yeah, well if he messes with us, he'll get hisself an ass full of lead."

The hand started to laugh.

But Raider didn't bother to smile. He figured to hang in there for a while. Keep his eyes open. And hope the damned renegade wasn't feeling lucky.

• • •

Big Bill reined up, dismounted, and knelt to look at the trail. "This is it, gentlemen. What we've been waitin' for."

They had stopped in a wooded area that Raider was sure he had seen before. Low forests. Lots of evergreens. The kind of place that a herd of elk might come to feed in the fall.

"I think I know where they are," Big Bill said. "This trail leads back to a runoff creek. If they're in there, we should be able to catch one without any trouble."

Raider gazed into the shadows between the trees. A great hiding place for Half Eagle. It was late afternoon, soon to be evening. He thought they should head back, but Big Bill was for pressing on.

"I need an elk for my smokehouse," he said. "It's tougher than most meat, but I can feed it to the hands."

Raider shook his head. "I ain't sure about this, Big Bill. It's gonna be dark soon. Maybe we oughta go see what Becky's got cookin' for dinner."

Walters ignored his caution and pointed upward. "There's a high trail through those trees. It circles around and looks down on a little ravine. Those animals got to cross through there to get to some meadows on the other side. I think we can catch 'em."

The hand said he would take the high path.

Raider waved him off. He wanted to go on the high trail, if there was no way of talking Walters out of the hunt. He figured it would give him a good vantage point to survey the area and see if Half Eagle was following them.

"All right," Walters said. "You go high, Raider. Me and this fellow'll stay on the low path. Now, if you see the herd, shoot at 'em and drive 'em back toward us. Or take the shot if you got it. But don't let 'em slip through that pass or we'll never find 'em."

Raider nodded. "Are you two goin' into the forest?"

"Don't worry," the hand replied. "The trail is clear. I'll stick with Mr. Walters."

"Be careful, Big Bill. If you see anybody in those trees, get the hell out."

Walters laughed. "You worry more'n Becky!"

"Just watch yourself."

Raider tied his mount and started up into the trees.

He was almost to the high path when he heard the cougar yowl.

Raider froze, listening for the second cry of the animal.

The mountain lion was probably after the herd, just like the hunters.

Raider considered running back down to the low path, to find Walters.

But he finally decided that he liked the high trail better.

He started to run, looking out for the cat that howled again somewhere in the forest.

The trees parted. Raider moved out to a ledge. He saw the elk below him. They were gathered around a pool, about twenty of them, having a drink from the crystal-clear water.

Suddenly a shot rang out.

One of the smaller bucks fell by the water.

The rest of the herd spooked and ran the other way.

Raider's black eyes squinted, searching for the puff of smoke in the diminishing light of the afternoon.

"Walters!" he called.

Big Bill called back. Raider saw him across the ravine, waving a hand. He had gotten the elk with one shot of his Sharps.

Raider waved back.

Then he heard the second shot.

Where the hell had it come from?

Big Bill buckled, tumbling to the ground, rolling down the slope toward the water. The rancher was crying out, screaming. Raider had to get to him. But how?

The way down was too steep if he tried to climb.

And it would take him another hour to backtrack.

Where the hell was the hired hand who had been with Walters?

Another shot rang out.

Who the hell was shooting at them?

Raider decided it was best to double back. He would be too good a target if he climbed. He just hoped he could make it to Big Bill while he was still alive.

As he turned, he saw something in the corner of his eye.

The shape was coming toward his head.

He tried to duck, but something caught him squarely on the temple.

Everything went black as he fell.

When he woke up, he had a hell of a headache.

The pain grew worse when he realized he was back at the lodge and Marshal Johnson was accusing him of shooting William Walters.

CHAPTER TWELVE

Things came back into focus too slowly. Raider felt the cool cloth on his forehead. Saw the outline of Becky's sweet face. She dipped the cloth in a bowl and dabbed it on his forehead again.

What the hell had happened?

He smelled the cedar logs of the lodge.

Back at Big Bill's.

Was it time for the big meeting?

That had come and gone.

Had something happened to Big Bill?

Becky leaned in closer, staring into his eyes. "Honey, it's me. Becky."

When he tried to nod, a sharp bolt of pain rushed through his head.

He fell back on the pallet of skins. The fire was roaring. He felt hot and sweaty.

He wanted to ask for whiskey but somebody pushed Becky away.

An unfamiliar face leaned in toward him "Why'd you shoot Big Bill?"

112   J. D. HARDIN

Raider didn't really hear it.

Becky tried to come back to his side.

The man pushed her away.

Raider wanted to get up and thrash the rude deputy, but the pain was too great in his head.

Somebody had hit him.

But where and why?

Marshal Bick Johnson leaned in over him. "Pinkerton, we found you in the bottom of that ravine, lyin' next to Big Bill. He was shot in the back and you were out cold."

He finally managed to squeak out the words. "Becky. Whiskey."

The blond girl pushed past the insolent lawmen. "Leave him alone. He didn't do anything to Big Bill."

The marshal glared at her and told her to go get the whiskey.

Then he looked at Raider again. "Somebody musta cold-cocked you, Pinkerton. You got a big lump on the back of your head."

Raider managed to touch the wound, wincing in the process.

Becky pushed in with the whiskey. "Will you get back. Give him air. He needs a drink."

Raider sipped from a whiskey bottle, feeling the rush of warmth that spread over his body.

He still didn't feel like talking.

But Johnson was full of words. "When you didn't come back, some of the hands tracked you to that ravine. Saw your horses tied up. Did you shoot Big Bill in the back, Pinkerton?"

Raider still couldn't believe he had been asked the question.

He wanted to speak.

But instead, he closed his eyes.

When he woke up again, he was still surrounded by lawmen in Big Bill's cedar lodge.

Johnson leaned in toward the big man from Arkansas. "You feelin' any better, Pinkerton?"

Raider was actually able to nod his head.

Becky edged by the marshal. "Can I get you anything, Raider?"

"Water," he said. "A pitcher of water."

His mouth was so dry that he drank most of the pitcher by himself.

Marshal Johnson seemed to be losing his patience. "Pinkerton, I need to know what happened out there. Did you see who shot Big Bill?"

Raider suddenly remembered the elk falling, then Walters tumbling down the incline. "He was shot in the back," the big man said. His eyes grew wide. "Is he—"

"He ain't dead," the marshal replied. "Not yet. He's lyin' upstairs asleep. The doctor's on the way."

Raider's head hurt again, a duller ache. "How about some more hooch?"

"The bottle's right there," Johnson offered. "But it put you to sleep last time."

Raider drank anyway. The whiskey took off the edge. He started to blink his eyes. He saw a puff of smoke. Big Bill's ambusher had been hiding back in the trees. But there was someone else. Swinging at him.

"There was two of 'em," he told the marshal. "One got Walters, the other one got me. I never saw it comin'. He musta knowed I was there all along."

The marshal squinted at him. "Wouldn't you've heard him comin'?"

"I can't re...no, I was runnin'. It woulda been easy for anybody to follow. I was lookin' for those elk. Then I was up top. Lookin' down at Big Bill. There was a shot. I turned and ...*bang*...I was hit."

Johnson still seemed skeptical. "We found you lyin' by that pool of water. You wasn't ten feet away from Big Bill."

Raider felt his head spinning. "Wait a minute. Do you think I shot him? Why the hell would I do a thing like that?"

Johnson appeared to have been thinking about that very question. "Well, I don't know. But you coulda shot him in the back. Then when you were goin' down to see if he was finished, you could've fell yourself and knocked your ownself silly."

Raider couldn't believe the lawman. "Why would I kill him?"

"He ain't dead yet," Johnson reminded him. "But it coulda been that you and the girl planned to take over the Double-W."

Becky glared at the marshal. "You ain't got a lick of sense, Bick Johnson. Raider and Big Bill were friends."

"Cain slew Abel," Johnson declared righteously. "And they were brothers."

Raider had another swallow of whiskey. He had been in this position before. At the mercy of an overworked lawman who was ready to accuse the first person who came along, just to make his job easier.

"Now I'm gonna ask you one more time," the marshal went on. "Did you shoot William Walters?"

"No."

Johnson exhaled. "Nevertheless, I did find you with Walters. And your gun had been fired. I must take you as the killer."

Raider felt a surge of anger, which seemed to take away the pain. "You thought I killed that minin' family too, but I didn't. You thought I was Rattler Rogers, but I wasn't. Seems like you'd get tired of bein' wrong, Johnson."

Johnson pointed at the big man. "Tie his hands. We're takin' him to Cheyenne, to the jailhouse."

Raider came off the skins, standing. His head spun a little. But he still had to take up for himself.

"Hear me out, Johnson. Me and Walters wasn't the only ones on that huntin' trip. There was a hired hand with us. He was the one who had seen the elk in the first place. Has he turned up?"

The marshal suddenly didn't seem so sure of himself. "A third man?"

Raider pointed toward the door. "Go ask the other hands if that man came back. It coulda been a trap all along."

Johnson told one of his men to go make inquiries.

While they waited, Becky brought Raider a shearling coat. "Here, honey, it's gettin' colder. Won't be long 'fore it starts snowin'."

Raider hefted the coat. It was too heavy. As he put it on, he felt iron in the pocket. Becky had slipped him a gun. She also pressed her body into his, to let him know that she also had a weapon under the folds of her skirt.

He peered into her eyes, trying to look severe. He didn't want to make a move with her involved. She might catch a stray piece of lead.

Johnson's deputy came back, saying that there had been a

third man along on the trip. That man had not returned yet. Nobody had seen him.

Johnson scratched his chin. "A third man, huh?"

"You owe me a look-see," Raider challenged. "We got to try to find the man who went with us. If he's still alive, maybe he can tell us somethin'."

The marshal nodded. "My men'll look for him. But you're goin' back to Cheyenne, Pinkerton."

Raider exchanged glances with Becky.

The girl understood him perfectly.

"Okay," he said. "I'll go. Just let me see Big Bill before I leave. You owe me that much, Johnson."

Johnson sighed. "All right, but I'm goin' with you."

Raider started toward Big Bill's room.

"He's in the loft," Becky said. "I had 'em put him up there."

Raider turned to go.

Johnson stopped him. "Just a minute, Pinkerton. Let me check that coat for sidearms."

Raider felt his gut starting to churn.

Johnson found the pistol in his coat, a pocket revolver no doubt taken from Big Bill's collection.

The marshal shook his head. "Shame on you, Pinkerton."

Raider hated lawmen. "I hate lawmen."

"Come on, let's go see Walters."

They went up the steps to the loft.

Becky came behind them.

Walters was lying under heavy covers. His eyes were closed. Ashen face. He looked so lifeless.

"Think the doctor can do anythin' for him?" Raider asked.

Johnson grabbed Raider's arm. "I don't know. I seen men killed by less and recovered from worse. But that ain't my problem now. That's between Walters and his Maker. Right now I got to get you back to Cheyenne."

"Can't you see what's gonna happen?" Raider pleaded. "Your boys couldn't find their asses with four hands and a' oil lamp. You got to let me stay on this thing, Marshal. I'm bettin' that Artis Blaylock and Dixon have somethin' to do with this."

Johnson shook his head. "Last I heard, Blaylock was on the

southbound stage. And I run Dixon out of town ever'time he shows up. I think you're wrong on this one, Pinkerton."

"You got to let me have a look around, Johnson."

Johnson stiffened, resting his hand on his revolver. "Better do like I say, Pinkerton. Now let's go."

"Raider ain't goin' nowhere with you, Marshal."

Becky had said it. She was standing behind Bick Johnson. Her hand was full of an old Army Colt. The one she had hidden under her skirt. Now the bore was pressed against the lawman's back.

"What the devil do you think you're doin', girl!"

Raider reached down and took the marshal's sidearm. "She's on my side, Bick. I hate to do this to you, but lie down on the floor."

The marshal reluctantly obeyed him. "This is gonna look bad for you, Pinkerton. You won't get away with it."

"Maybe not," Raider replied. "But don't take it personal, Bick. I just don't want to rot in that jail of yourn, not while I can go out and find the man who really shot Big Bill."

He started for the window.

"Go out the back way," Becky said. "There's a horse there. I had Pepe bring it for you."

He winked at her. "If I had more time, honey. I'd kiss you."

"Just find out who shot Big Bill," the girl said.

Raider assured her that he would.

He slid out on the roof and started stepping sideways.

Most of Johnson's men were inside or on the front porch. Nobody out back. Just the horse that Becky had left him.

Raider swung off the eave of the roof, dropping to the ground. The mountain was high overhead behind him. No moon, not yet anyway.

He untied the reins of a tall stallion.

Becky cried out upstairs.

The marhsal's voice rose up. "The Pinkerton has escaped!"

Johnson appeared at the window above him.

Raider swung into the saddle.

Johnson pointed the weapon he had taken away from Becky.

He fired one shot.

But it missed.

Raider rounded the lodge, driving for the dark, moonless plain.

The ground began to slope upward.

There was a bright round moon rising behind him.

Raider reined back when he found the place where Walters and the hired hand had gotten onto the low path. He followed the trail, keeping his horse behind him. The going was slow and rough.

What the hell would he find in the moonlight?

He remembered the third shot in the trees. The hand had been killed as well. Two men after them. Was Half Eagle involved? Maybe the Indian had a whole band of men.

Then why hadn't he killed Raider?

Better to frame the big Pinkerton, watch him hang for a murder he didn't commit. Damned clever for a renegade—if it was Half Eagle behind the scheme.

Raider thanked God that Big Bill hadn't died.

He had to stop on the trail, taking his bearings. How long had he been out? It would have taken Johnson a day to get to the Double-W from Cheyenne. A day for somebody to go after him.

The moon seemed to be racing across the sky.

He stayed on the trail for a long time, taking it slow, listening.

Something rustled ahead of him.

Then he heard the yowling of a mountain cat.

He remembered the same sound from before.

The cat was just above him.

Raider drew his Colt and fired in the general direction of the cougar.

Noise in the trees as the animal bounded away.

Raider then realized that he could hear running water. He was near the ravine. He started to take a step and then the smell hit him. He walked on, getting closer.

The stallion reared again.

"You smell it too."

Raider almost tripped over the body that lay across the middle of the trail. The cougar had been feeding on the dead man's guts. He forced himself to strike a match. It was the hired hand all right. His throat had been cut.

Raider drew back from the body. He wished he had time to give the man a decent burial. But he had to get out of the woods in a hurry, before the marshal caught up with him.

He rose in a wide circle, doubling back to the line of the lower ranges. Johnson would come after him, because he would figure out that Raider had gone back to the ravine looking for the hired man. Raider had to wonder if the body had been placed across the trail deliberately. It surely hadn't been there when Big Bill's men came looking for them. Was it a blatant manipulation? Or had the cougar found it and dragged it out of the trees?

He followed the foothills until he could see the lodge.

He dismounted and found a way to get closer on foot. He wanted to see if the marshal had taken all his men. Surely Johnson wouldn't figure him to double back to the lodge.

From a hiding place in the rocks, he peered toward the house.

Only one light burned in the loft.

He couldn't see the front porch.

He leaned back, waiting for the sun.

His eyes closed.

When he awoke, he heard the echoes of a rattling buggy harness.

The sun was up.

Raider thought the buggy belonged to Artis Blaylock. But then he saw the black bag in the man's hand when he climbed off the driver's seat. The doctor. And there didn't seem to be any horses in front of the lodge.

He came out of the rocks, clutching Marshal Johnson's Remington.

Nobody seemed to take notice of his approach. The early hands had already risen, and the night riders were asleep. He hesitated at the back door, listening. Nobody in the kitchen. He eased in, listening.

The main parlor was empty.

Had Johnson taken all of his deputies to look for the fugitive?

When he reached the top step, he heard voices. Becky was talking to the doctor. Then the physician replied that she should keep Big Bill warm. Just watch him and pray. The bullet had gone straight through him so there was no way to tell how much damage had been done. Big Bill might recover. He might not.

Raider slipped into the room, brandishing the six-gun. "Don't move."

The doctor's eyes grew wide.

Raider tried to smile. "Sorry, Doc. I ain't got nothin' agin you. But I'm afraid I'm gonna have to ask you for your hat and coat."

Becky came toward him. "Raider, you're..."

He waved her away. "Stay with Big Bill, honey. Make sure he gets better. He needs you more'n I do."

The doctor was frozen.

Raider waved the barrel of the pistol. "You're gonna stay here too, Doc. Leastways till the marshal comes back. See, Johnson is gonna think I killed that man in the woods. You tell him I said I didn't. Tell him I'm gonna find out who did. Now take off that coat and hat."

The man was smaller than Raider, so the disguise would fit pretty tight.

"I'll have to take your buggy too, sir. But I'm really a' honest Pinkerton and you'll get it back or as much as what its worth. And you take care of Big Bill. Go on, take it off."

The doctor removed his hat and coat.

"Now," Raider told him. "I'm gonna have to tie you up, but Becky'll cut you loose when I'm gone. I'll empty your bag before I take it with me. And I swear you'll have it back."

Becky threw her arms around him. "Love me once before you go."

He pressed his lips against hers, wondering if it would be their last kiss.

Becky wanted more.

"I don't have time," he told her. "I gotta go. You stay here. I'll be in touch if I need you."

"Tell me you love me, Raider."

He hesitated.

"I don't care if you do or not," Becky went on. "Just tell me."

"I love you, Becky."

"I love you too. And if you get out of this, I promise I'm gonna marry you. I promise."

He tried to smile again. "I'll hold you to that. Now, help me get this coat on."

The doctor's coat and hat fit him better than he thought it would.

When he picked up the bag, he glanced at Becky and asked, "How do I look?"

She nodded, but she couldn't talk. Tears streamed down her face. She seemed to be choking on the words.

Raider couldn't stay to console her.

He went downstairs, pausing by the window to look out onto the front porch. Johnson had left one man behind. Raider could see his badge.

He opened the front door and started out.

"How's Walters?" the sentry asked.

Raider didn't look straight at him. "Fine." He tried to keep walking.

"Hey, you're not the doctor. You're the Pink—"

Raider swung and hit him squarely between the eyes.

The deputy went down and stayed there.

Raider's hand stung.

But he couldn't slow down.

He had to keep moving.

He climbed onto the buggy and grabbed the reins, swinging in a wide circle, heading back south. The horse wasn't very fast, but it was steady. Raider just hoped like hell that he didn't run into Marshal Johnson along the way.

CHAPTER THIRTEEN

When the messages from Raider stopped coming at regular intervals, Wagner really didn't worry any more than usual. He figured the hard-bitten cowboy had lapsed back into his old habits. He expected another case-ending message to the effect that Raider was no longer working for William Walters.

Wagner was shocked by the next wire he received from Wyoming. It came two weeks after the so called "caucus" that had been reported in the newspapers, even the publications in Chicago. He had been planning to pull Raider off the case. And then the message came in.

The telegraph operator brought it himself. "Another one from Wyomin'. It's about Raider."

Wagner's eyes grew wide as he read it. "My word!"

He went directly to Allan Pinkerton's office and knocked on the door.

Pinkerton looked up when Wagner barged in. "It's not like you to be rude, William."

"Raider's in trouble."

Pinkerton leaned forward, forgetting all about his associate's unexpected intrusion. "Let me see."

He read the telegram. "Attempted murder, horse thievery, flight from an officer of the law."

"It's the same marshal who wrongly arrested Raider before," Wagner offered. "Johnson."

Pinkerton dropped the telegram on his desk. He leaned back and rubbed his eyes. This was his decision to make. Wagner knew it too.

"Where's Stokes?" Pinkerton asked.

"Kansas. I heard from him yesterday."

The burly Scotsman nodded. "Send him."

"Anyone else?"

Pinkerton looked at his second-in-command. "What did you have in mind, William?"

"Anderson. I think he's ready for something like this."

Pinkerton chortled derisively. "Raider'll more'n likely get him killed. You think Anderson is ready for the big hooligan's roughhousing?"

"Stokes will be there."

Pinkerton waved him toward the door. "Have 'em meet in Denver."

Wagner nodded and hurried out of the office.

The telegraph man was still waiting. He understood the importance of the reply. It would take Wagner a while to compose his directives. Of course, the newest addition to the agency, a young man named Anderson, was in Chicago, so he could be sent right away. Stokes might have to wait for him in Denver.

Wagner shook off his frustrations. Raider was running true to form. He was daft to think the tall brute would ever shape up. Sometimes he was more trouble than he was worth.

"Got your reply, Mr. Wagner?"

He realized the key operator was still there.

Wagner leaned back and looked at him. "You're enjoying all this, aren't you, sir?"

The man blushed a little. "Well, you got to admit that Raider is pretty colorful."

"To say the least."

"And," the man offered. "I don't think he did all those things they say."

Wagner sighed. "That remains to be seen."

"I can't wait to see how it all turns out, Mr. Wagner."

"Neither can I, sir. Neither can I."

CHAPTER FOURTEEN

As Raider rolled south, handling the reins of the buggy, he considered his next move. It would be suicide to head back to Cheyenne. Even in the doctor's coat and hat, it wouldn't take someone long to spot the tall Pinkerton in Marshal Johnson's domain. Besides, he didn't have to go Cheyenne anyway. The man he wanted had headed south on the stagecoach.

Johnson had said it. Blaylock left town on the stage. Southbound. That meant Denver, or one of the towns along the way. Hell, there weren't many towns on the road to Denver, so Blaylock had to be heading for the mile-high settlement.

Raider wondered if Blaylock had taken Dixon with him. The marshal hadn't said if the bushwhacker had gone with Blaylock. Maybe they'd meet up on the trail somewhere. Or maybe Blaylock had shed himself of the brutish Dixon. That would be the wise thing to do. Dixon would stick out anywhere, even in a place like Denver.

Raider kept on, heading south as fast as the buggy would carry him. He wished that he had Big Bill's stallion to ride. The black was a whole lot faster. But the buggy would have to do, at least until he could find another mount.

He had to stop every five or six miles to rest the harness-bred.

A cold wind had begun to blow down from the north, the first sign of the snow that might follow. Raider dug into his pockets, looking for money. He still had more than a hundred dollars in back pay, even after he had reimbursed Walters for the expense money.

He grieved when he thought about Big Bill, lying there in that bed. He prayed that the rancher would wake up. Not because he wanted to clear his own name, but because he didn't want to lose a friend. Big Bill didn't deserve his fate. He hadn't done anything wrong. But that was how it went sometimes. Good men just got it in the gut.

During one of his rest stops, Raider searched around in the back of the buggy, hoping to find something useful. The doctor kept bandages and tinctures stacked neatly in the storage compartment. There was also a small can of black powder and some matches.

Raider closed the compartment and turned south. He had to reach a stage stop, to find out if Blaylock had continued this way. If Blaylock was really behind the shooting of Walters, then he might fake a departure to divert suspicion away from himself.

Blaylock had to be at fault. Who else wanted Big Bill out of the way? Did Blaylock really think that Big Bill's demise would shift sentiment away from statehood?

Of course, there was always the possibility that the renegade, Half Eagle, had shot Big Bill. But that would have to wait. Raider figured he had to find Blaylock first. Then he could make a decision about how to proceed with the investigation.

The first night, he had to camp on the plain.

He shot a rabbit with Marshal Johnson's Remington. The meat was tough after he turned it over the fire. But he had to eat to stay strong.

The next day, he found a stage stop, but the station man didn't remember seeing Blaylock. Said he never took much notice of the passengers unless they were pretty women. Raider bought a bowl of stew from the man and went on his way.

By late afternoon, he saw the sign that read FORT COLLINS, TEN MILES.

He could make it by nightfall.

Maybe buy a horse.

Get rid of the buggy that was slowing him down.

He rolled into town well after dark, so the stage depot was closed.

Raider found a resting place for the buggy and went to sleep.

The next morning, when he opened his eyes, there were blue-coated soldiers all around him.

Had word of his escape already reached this far south?

A captain stood over him. "Good mornin', sir."

Raider nodded, thinking that this was the end. "How do."

The captain gestured toward the buggy. "One of my men noticed a doctor's bag on your vehicle."

What could he do but nod again?

The captain smiled. "I have a man who's in need of medical attention. Could you be of some help?"

Raider felt his stomach beginning to protest.

But what else could he do? If he refused to treat the man, the soldiers might become suspicious. So he told them to lead the way.

They took him to the fort, where the man lay back on a cot.

His arm had been sliced open by a knife.

"He got into a fight," the captain said. "I suppose I should reprimand him, but the other man started it."

Raider looked at the wound, trying to appear genuine. "I've seen worse, sir. Don't you have a doctor here at the fort?"

The captain smiled, shaking his head. "Well, we did. But he retired a few weeks ago and went back east. I'm always reluctant to consult the local physician. He has a habit of drinking too much."

Raider stood up. "Well, let me get to my stuff. I'll see what I can do. That cut goes all the way up his arm, and it's startin' to fester. But I think I can help him."

Raider returned to the wagon, nervously going through the doctor's inventory of cures. He picked up several alcohol tinctures, but then his eye caught the black powder. He figured the powder would work as good as anything else.

The wounded man groaned when he came back. "Doc, am I gonna lose my arm?"

"No," Raider replied. "Not if I can help it."

The captain grimaced when he saw the black powder. "What are you going to do with that, sir?"

"You'll see."

Raider asked the captain to give his man a bullet, something to bite on.

When the lead was between the man's teeth, Raider poured black powder in the trench of the wound. "This is gonna hurt, pardner."

The wounded man braced himself.

The captain turned away.

Raider struck a match and lit the powder. A stream of sparks shot up the man's arm. He screamed as the trail burned the length of the wound.

When the powder had burned out, Raider asked for wet cloths. He washed the wound and then poured a tincture on it. After wrapping the wound with fresh bandages, he figured there was nothing more that he could do.

"You aren't going to stitch it up?" the captain asked.

Raider shrugged. "It's not deep enough. My guess is that he was cut with a dirty knife. But it should be okay. Change the bandage every day and keep putting this on it."

He gave the captain a tincture.

The officer thanked him and asked what Raider required as payment.

Raider considered asking for a mount, but he figured that it might seem suspicious if he gave up the buggy. "You don't owe me a thing, Captain. I'm happy just to help a man in uniform."

"Serve in the Army did you?"

"No, sir. Can't say as I had the pleasure. But I have respect for the Army. Lots of it."

The captain escorted him outside. "Well, I suppose my sergeant will think twice before he tangles with local riffraff like Dixon."

Raider tried not to seem eager. "Dixon?"

"Yes, this local brute. Comes down from Wyoming sometimes. Godless territory up there."

Raider nodded. "Yeah," he said, feeling his heart inside his chest, "I ain't much on it myself."

"Tell me," the captain said, "did you study medicine at a university?"

"Er, no. I sort of studied on it by myself."

"Well, I suppose that's what makes the West a great place. Ingenuity. I'll take ingenuity any day."

Raider nodded in agreement. But he only had two things on his mind. Getting away from the fort and finding Harley Dixon.

The station man at the Fort Collins depot remembered Blaylock, but he had no recollection of Harley Dixon. Blaylock had been passing through to Denver. But Dixon had not been traveling with him.

"Why you want to know?" the man asked.

"They both owe me money," Raider replied. "I treated 'em back in Cheyenne, but they skipped out."

"Prob'ly find them in Denver."

"I hope so."

Raider went outside, back to the buggy. He had to get rid of the slow vehicle if he was going to get to Denver in a hurry. He was wondering what to do when he heard a ruckus inside the depot.

Somebody was complaining in a loud voice. "Whatta you mean the northbound stage don't come through for another week?"

Raider looked in the door to see a man and a woman in front of the depot man's desk.

"My wife and me got to get to Cheyenne!"

"I'm sorry," the station man replied. "There's nothin' I can do."

The man kept on, but he was finally discouraged by the station man's persistence. The stage wouldn't be back for a week. That was the long and short of it. There was nothing the depot man could do.

The traveler stormed out of the depot with his wife in his tracks. "Dad-blamed stage line." Then, to his spouse: "Well, honey, I reckon we're stuck in Colorado for another week."

Raider took a step toward the disgruntled wayfarer. "Not necessarily, sir."

The man gaped at him. "Hell, pardner, I got just enough money for two stage tickets. And that ain't enough to buy one horse, let alone two."

Raider smiled. "Well, seems like we both got trouble. I need to get that buggy back to Cheyenne, but I also got to head west. And there ain't no way I can do both at the same time."

The traveler didn't seem to catch on right away. "What's that got to do with me?"

Raider gestured toward the buggy. "Well, I'll let you take the buggy if you promise me you'll deliver it to my brother. See, he's the doctor in Cheyenne. But I got business west of here, in Boulder."

He had to lie. Didn't want Marshal Johnson to know he was heading for Denver. Throw the lawman off the trail, at least for a while. He figured Johnson wouldn't be too hard on the traveler, not if he delivered the stolen buggy back to the doctor.

"You think you can trust me?" the man asked.

Raider shrugged. "Well, I'll just send a wire north, to the marshal. If you don't turn up in a week or so, you'll be in a heap of trouble. They still hang horse thieves in this part of the country."

"As well they should!" the man replied.

His wife seemed reluctant. "Don't do it, Caleb."

"Hush up, woman." He nodded to Raider. "All right. I'll deliver the buggy. But what's it gonna cost me?"

"Just your name and the name of any kin you got in Wyomin'," Raider said. "That way, I can track you down if you don't do what I ask."

"Caleb. Caleb Struthers. And I got a cousin in Cheyenne. Name's Jim Struthers."

Raider gestured toward the buggy. "She's all yours, Struthers. Get it back to Cheyenne in one piece and you'll have a friend for life."

They shook hands.

Raider strode quickly away, hoping to find a stable. He wanted to buy a new horse. A strong animal that would get him to Denver in a hurry.

Raider stood across the street from the Sundowner Hotel in Denver, watching the main entrance.

Artis Blaylock had not been hard to find. City men left too many traces behind them. Blaylock had been staying at the Sundowner for more than a week. Raider had bribed the desk clerk for the information.

Blaylock had also been entertaining three men from time to time. Sharing whiskey in his room. The desk clerk identified the three men by appearance and last name—Carlton, Davis, and Wages. He also promised to keep Raider's inquiry a secret.

So far, the man named Wages was the only one Raider had been able to track down. He was a railroad man. New to Colorado. Hoped to open a line north, into Wyoming. Raider wondered if the rail man had anything to do with Blaylock's stand against statehood for the territory just north of Colorado. Would the railroad scheme benefit in some way from the breakup of the Wyoming territory?

Raider would just have to stay on the job if he wanted to find out.

He pulled the doctor's coat tighter over his chest.

The weather had turned sour. Cold air swept down from the north, bringing flurries of snow. He would have bought a new coat, but the new mount, including a saddle, and the bribes to the desk clerk had drained him. He barely had enough left to pay for sleeping in the loft where he stabled his mount.

He considered wiring the home office for more money. But by now, Wagner probably knew the big man was on the run. He wouldn't send a silver dollar to Raider, not as long as he was an outlaw.

He just had to stay with it until he could uncover the truth.

Raider straightened up when Artis Blaylock came out of the hotel.

Two men flanked Blaylock. They were laughing. All three of them started down the sidewalk.

Raider followed them until they entered a storefront. He stopped across the street, trying to hang back in the shadows. Word of his flight from Cheyenne might have reached the authorities in Denver. No need to flee one jail just to get locked up in another one.

He peered toward the window of the office. COLORADO RAIL COMPANY had been painted across the glass. Raider knew from experience that different states and territories had laws governing the railroads. Maybe it would be easier for Wages if the southern regions of Wyoming were absorbed by the territory of Colorado. It made sense that the railroad would have an easier time laying tracks in the flat part of Wyoming, on the plain.

He shook off the chill. It was only two weeks into November, but the winter cold had already taken over. He's have to find a way to get money for a warmer coat.

After an hour or so, Blaylock came out of the office with one of the men. They headed for another office that read EZEKIEL DAVIS, LAND SURVEYOR. Was Blaylock making preparations for the breakup of the territory? Was he that confident of failure for the cause of statehood?

Damn it all, Raider thought, Blaylock had to know about the attempt on Big Bill's life. Maybe Walters was already dead. That would make Raider a suspect in a murder case.

Blaylock came out again, striding back toward the hotel.

Raider watched him enter.

The cold air rushed around his head.

Blaylock had to have a weakness, something Raider could exploit.

He would just have to keep after the man, watch him, pray for an opening.

It came along when Blaylock went to see the woman.

Raider was familiar with the part of Denver that was famous for the ladies of the evening.

At first, he was surprised that Blaylock would frequent the seedy side of town, but then it seemed to made sense. What other kind of woman would have anything to do with the weasel-eyed businessman? Blaylock wasn't much to look at. And he didn't seem to have much charm.

So Raider stayed on his tail, keeping in the shadows, following him to the back alleys where whores plied their trade.

He watched from behind a rain barrel as Blaylock climbed the steps and knocked on the door.

A blond-haired woman let him in. Raider tried to get a look at her face. It would be easier to get information out of her if he had been with her before. But he could barely get a glimpse of her before the door closed again.

Blaylock stayed with her for a long time. Almost three hours. By Denver standards, the whore would probably charge him twenty dollars. Blaylock seemed to be a man of means.

It was almost dark before Blaylock came down the stairs again.

Raider waited a few minutes and then went up to the closed door, knocking loudly.

The blond woman gawked when she saw him. "Raider!"

His eyes grew wide. "Lolly?"

"You remembered. Come on in, boy. It's been a long time."

Raider smiled, thinking that his job was going to be a whole lot easier.

"I ain't got no money, Lolly."

She shrugged. "So? I been known to give one free to a' old friend. How did you find me? I moved from my old place."

"A friend of mine," he replied. "That boy who was here before me. I thought he was never gonna leave."

Lolly shook her head, grimacing. She didn't look bad. Her breasts were bigger and she had added a few inches to her hips. But she still had a smile for him.

"He treat you right?" Raider asked.

"Artis? Hell, I don't even know why he comes to see me. Mostly he just talks. Then he jumps on me and blows his load. Always wants to do it right before he leaves."

Raider sat down in a wooden chair. "That right?"

She asked him if he wanted a drink.

Raider said he could use a snort and something to eat if she had it. He would pay her later. After he got his back pay.

Lolly eyed him carefully. "You look different. Where's your Stetson?"

He shrugged. "I got to buy me a new one when I get the money."

"You still a Pinkerton?"

He nodded. "Yeah. I reckon."

She handed him a shot glass full of whiskey. "It's a little rough goin' down, but it gets the job done."

After a few snorts, Raider looked into her green eyes. "So, my friend Artis is a talker, huh?"

"Lordy yes. Goes on about how rich he's gonna be after

the Colorado border is pushed north. Somethin' about railroads and land. I never listen to most of it. Seems like he thinks the territory of Wyomin' is gonna be broke up soon."

That was all Raider needed to hear. "Well, Lolly, looks like I done took up enough of your time."

He started to get up.

Lolly pushed him back into the chair. "What's your hurry?"

He couldn't tell her that he had to get back on Blaylock's trail, to prove that he had been behind the shooting of Big Bill Walters. She would probably tell Blaylock that Raider had been there, so that made time precious. He had to poke around before Blaylock came back to see her.

Lolly knelt down in front of him. "I never knowed you to run away from a willin' woman, Raider. Don't tell me that you've changed. Has workin' for Mr. Pinkerton made you soft?"

"Lolly, I told you, I ain't got no money."

Her hand began to rub his crotch. "And I told you that it don't matter. I always liked you, Raider. You know how to treat a woman, at least most of the time. Here, let me take it out."

He figured it would just be easier to go ahead and do it. Besides, he suddenly felt ready. His jeans were tighter around the crotch.

Lolly went to work on the buttons of his fly. "Let's see what you got here."

She pulled his cock out of his pants.

"Mmm," she cooed. "As big as ever."

She stroked him up and down.

Raider gestured toward the bed. "Wouldn't it be better over there?"

She smiled at him. "You got to get undressed first. Here, stand up, let me get your clothes off."

Lolly undressed him slowly, teasing him all the way. By the time she finally got his boots off, he was aching to have her. Lolly dropped to her knees, taking his prick into hand.

"Some cowboys don't like the Frenchy stuff," she said, looking up at him with her big green eyes. "But I know you do."

"Lolly..."

"Oh, let a girl have a treat, Raider!"

Her lips closed on the end of his cock. She took him in and out, working on him with her mouth and tongue. Raider felt the load rising.

"Lolly, I'm gonna shoot."

But she kept on anyway.

He shivered with his release.

Lolly held still, swallowing his fiery offering.

When she was finished, she stood up. "That was good. I don't do it for many men, but I just felt the urge when I saw you, Raider."

"Well, I reckon I oughta thank you."

She grabbed his prick and dragged him toward the bed. "Now you just settle down in them sheets."

"Lolly..."

He had to get going.

"I thought you was hungry," she offered. "Don't you want me to feed you? Hell, you fed me."

He fell back on the bed, figuring it was better than the cold loft he had been sleeping in.

"I can't stay long," he told her.

"Well, you better stay long enough to get hard again. I want some of that thing between my legs."

She went across the room, opening the door of a potbellied stove. She threw two logs into the fire and then put a pan on top of the heater. Raider nodded when she asked him if he liked soup.

After they had eaten, Lolly slipped into bed with him. It didn't take long to get him fully erect. She fell back, spreading her legs.

"Give it to me, honey."

Raider rolled over, slipping between her legs. He prodded her moist crotch, trying to get it in. Lolly helped him by guiding the prickhead to the entrance of her cunt.

"All the way," she told him.

Raider drove his cock to the hilt.

Lolly gasped, lifting her legs toward the ceiling. "That feels good. Ain't no cowboys can... ohh..."

He had a little trouble getting the second release, but that seemed to be all right with Lolly. She rocked with him, enjoying every thrust. When she felt his cock expanding with the rush of his climax, she told him to pull out.

Raider withdrew, discharging on her stomach.

Lolly grabbed his prick, milking the last drop, running her fingers through the jism. "You know how to fuck, Raider."

He rolled off her. "I reckon."

She kept her hand on his cock, hoping he would get hard again.

Raider wanted to go, to stay after Blaylock, but the damned bed felt too soft and warm.

"Close your eyes," Lolly told him. "I'll let you stay for a while. Tuesday is usually a slow day."

Raider didn't have the strength to protest. He lay back, pulling the covers over his nakedness. He slept soundly until he heard the knocking on the door.

As he raised up, he saw Lolly lighting a candle. "Just a minute," she called. "Hold your horses."

The door swung open.

A man came in.

"Lolly, I'm sorry to bother you, but I was wondering if . . ."

Artis Blaylock looked straight at Raider.

The big man from Arkansas grinned at the weasel-eyed businessman. "Hello, Artis. I bet you wasn't expectin' to see me."

The look in Blaylock's eyes told Raider that he was right.

CHAPTER FIFTEEN

Artis Blaylock lurched toward the open door.

Raider came off the bed, lunging for him, grabbing him by the scruff of the collar. He was sorry Blaylock had seen him, but since it was over, he had to make the best of the unfortunate circumstances. Dragging the slender businessman back into the room, he slammed the door and then pinned Blaylock against it.

"Why you runnin', Artis?"

Raider was right up in his weasel-face.

"You're a wanted man," Blaylock squeaked.

"How you know that? You left Cheyenne before Bill Walters was shot."

Blaylock's face went slack. "You shot Walters?"

Raider bounced him off the door. "No, somebody else did. And you know who shot him, don't you, Artis?"

"No! I swear."

"It was your man Dixon. Wasn't it?"

Blaylock was frozen. His mouth trembled, and sweat had broken on his brow. Raider could feel his slim frame as it shook from fear.

Lolly cowered by the potbellied stove, gaping at them. "I thought y'all was friends."

Raider began to pat down Blaylock, looking for a pistol. "Artis and I go way back. He did a friend of mine dirty. Whoa, what's this, Artis?"

He found a pocket revolver inside Blaylock's coat. Raider hadn't given him time to draw it. He rested the bore of the pistol on Blaylock's nose. The man's face turned pale.

"You wouldn't!" Blaylock moaned.

Raider's eyes narrowed and he forced a jack-o'-lantern grimace. "You know who shot Big Bill."

"No!"

"Who's Big Bill?" Lolly asked.

Raider told her to be quiet. Then he told her to get her coat and leave. He didn't want Lolly involved in any of this. Better if she stayed away till he was finished with Blaylock.

When she was gone, he turned back to the trembling man who now sat on the edge of Lolly's bed. "You was comin' back to set up Lolly with your friends. Ain't that it, Blaylock?"

"What friends?"

Raider scowled at him. "You know, Carlton, Davis, and Wages—the men you're doin' business with."

Blaylock was speechless.

"Yeah, I know all about it. One's for the railroad. And the surveyor. And what's the other one? A rancher or a miner?"

Blaylock looked down at the floor.

"You had to have Big Bill shot, didn't you, Artis?"

"Never."

"Then how'd you know I was wanted up in Wyomin'?"

Blaylock shrugged. "Somebody told me."

"I'm bettin' it was Dixon. Was he the one who pulled the trigger? Or was he the one who knocked me out?"

Nothing from the hangdog businessman.

Raider suddenly realized that he was naked. He kept the pistol in his hand while he dressed. It was hard pulling on his boots. Blaylock really didn't offer any resistance. He seemed to be pondering something.

Raider started in again. "If Dixon hit me, then that means you pulled the trigger on Big Bill. And you cut the hired man's throat."

"None of that is true, I tell you!"

"Can you prove it ain't?"

Blaylock's eyes grew wide. He seemed to stiffen. "Yes, I can prove every word. Unequivocally!"

Raider wasn't sure about the last word, but he still figured to call Blaylock's bluff. "I'm ready to listen," he said. "But somethin' tells me you ain't got shit, Artis."

Blaylock stood up. "In my hotel room. I can prove that I didn't have anything to do with shooting Walters."

Raider waved the barrel of the pocket revolver. "This better be good."

"I assure you, I'm innocent. *You're* the one who's on the run from the law, Pinkerton!"

Raider felt like smacking him. But he knew he had to listen to Blaylock. Like it or not, there was always a possibility that Blaylock was innocent.

"I'm gonna be hard to convince," he said as he ushered the slim man down the steps.

"You're going to be surprised, Pinkerton."

And he sure as hell was.

Raider kept the gun in Blaylock's back as they approached the hotel.

The desk clerk looked up when they entered the small lobby. His face was white. Raider squinted at the young man, wondering if he had seen the pocket revolver against Blaylock's spine.

"What the hell?"

The big man froze. Something was wrong. The desk clerk ducked behind the counter.

Raider heard rifle levers chortling.

Suddenly five men had the drop on him. They came out of the shadows, through closed doors. Someone slipped a gun in Raider's back. A standoff.

"Drop the gun," said a familiar voice.

Raider let go of the pocket revolver. "Hello, Johnson."

Blaylock lurched away from the big man. "You fool. I led you straight to him. Now you'll hang in Wyoming!" He turned and fled to his room.

Marshal Bick Johnson moved around to face Raider.

One of his men picked up the pocket revolver.

Raider exhaled defeatedly. "Was it the doctor's buggy?"

Johnson shook his head. "No, we met him on the trail, but we were already heading this way. By the way, the doc'll appreciate the gesture. I know he'll be glad to get his buggy back."

"How's Big Bill?"

Johnson's face went slack. "Still alive, last I heard. You shot him, didn't you, Raider?"

The big man ignored the question. "How'd you figure out where to find me, Marshal?"

"Made sense that you'd run after Blaylock. He was the one you suspected. But you shot Big Bill didn't you?"

Raider fought back the rage that welled inside him. No sense taking on five deputies. Keep it inside, so he could use it later.

"We found Blaylock," Johnson went on. "Luck would have it that we found you."

He started to push Raider toward the door.

"Goin' back on the stage?" Raider asked.

They went outside.

The deputies fell in on both sides of him.

"Gonna ride back," the marshal told him. "I hate the stage."

"So do I," Raider offered. "Gonna tie my hands?"

"Chains. I can't trust you, Raider. You done escaped from me once. Go on and tell me if you shot Big Bill."

But Raider's wasn't having any of the marshal's stupidity.

Two weeks in the Cheyenne jailhouse and there still wasn't any word from Wagner. Johnson had sent the telegraph message as Raider requested, but the reply had not yet arrived. They had ridden from Denver in less time.

Raider was being held for murdering the hired hand and for wounding Big Bill. The old boy still clung to life. Becky came to see Raider every week after she learned that he was in Cheyenne. Usually she arrived on Sunday with a picnic basket and word from the ranch.

Some of Walters's hired hands were convinced that Raider had killed their boss. They were angry about it. Came into town and drank a lot, shot their mouths off.

But Big Bill was fine. He was sitting up. Taking broth. His eyes were open, but he seemed addled. He couldn't talk yet.

Raider was glad that he was alive.

Which was more than he would be able to say for himself in a little while.

Johnson had been waiting for the circuit judge to return from Rock Springs. He had promised Raider a fair trial. The big man figured he had a good case, what with Half Eagle on the loose. Unless the jury decided to believe the marshal. Damn it, he needed a lawbook thumper.

Why the hell hadn't Wagner sent one?

Maybe the wire was down.

Maybe Johnson had lied about sending the message.

Raider would have to tell Becky to send another wire when she came on Sunday. Why hadn't he thought of that in the first place? He was slipping. And the damned cards had fallen so strangely. The perfect ambush.

Maybe Wagner had something else cooked up. Something big. He had to know Raider was in trouble.

Johnson came in with Raider's dinner.

"Any word?" the big man asked.

The marshal frowned and shook his head. "The judge will be in next week. But I'm not so sure we'll have a trial."

Raider grimaced. "Just gonna lynch me outright?"

Johnson slid the tray under the cell door. "I want to talk a spell while you eat your dinner."

Raider went to work on the fried chicken. "A man in my position ain't in any position to quarrel, Johnson."

The marshal sat in a wooden chair that rested against the planked wall. "I been thinkin'..."

"Always dangerous for a lawman."

Johnson raised an eyebrow. "You want to hear this?"

"I do if it means I'll walk free."

"All right," the marshal continued, "I got to thinkin'. The renegade is hidin' up there. He coulda killed that man and shot Walters."

"Marshal—"

Johnson pointed a finger at him. "Let me finish."

He nodded, lowering his head. "I'm listenin'."

He wanted to get the hell out of the jailhouse.

Johnson took a deep breath. "See, I went back up there. I went up on that ledge, the one where you said you were watchin' when Big Bill was shot. I found this."

He took something out of his pocket.

Raider peered at the empty brass cartridge that had come from a Winchester rifle. It was the big bullet, the one for his '76. Someone had fired his rifle on the ledge.

"I got to thinkin'," Johnson said. "Why would Raider have shot at Big Bill from way up here? And I saw that elk carcass. Critters had been feedin' on it, but I was able to figure out where Big Bill had shot from. It didn't make sense. I mean, you just wouldn'ta shot from there."

Raider nodded, wiping his mouth with the back of his hand. "Congratulations, Marshal. You just learned the difference between bein' a lawman and bein' a detective. I'm tellin' you, I was cold-cocked up there."

"You did have a bump on your head."

"I saw Big Bill drop. Somebody shot from behind. I didn't see the smoke from the gun, so it must've been high up. That hired hand had already been killed by then."

Johnson rubbed his chin. "It sure might've happened that way."

"It was Dixon!" Raider cried. "He was workin' for Blaylock. And Blaylock might've been the one to pull the trigger on Big Bill."

"Why do you keep harpin' on Blaylock?"

Raider grabbed the bars of the cell. "Don't you see? Blaylock's the only one who spoke against Big Bill and statehood. He's thrown in with some men in Colorado. I think they want to see the border of Colorado pushed north. They'd like to see the territory divied up."

Johnson glared at him. "How the devil did you figure all this out?"

"I just did. Like I said before, it's the difference between the lawman and the Pink. One sees what he wants. The other sees what's there."

"You sayin' I ain't one to do justice?"

Raider turned away, exhaling. "You ain't done justice by me."

"You ran to Denver, Pinkerton!"

"Yeah, and I guess I knew you'd have enough sense to follow me. But I went anyway. Hell, if I'da wanted you to lose my trail, you'da never found me, Marshal. I'm that good."

Johnson stood up. "Listen, I'm gonna have to keep you locked up till the judge gets here. Then I'll sit down with him and see what he thinks about all this."

Raider spun back toward the lawman. "Johnson! I want my say with the judge. I want a chance to prove myself innocent."

"For what it's worth," the marshal offered, "I think you are innocent. We'll just have to wait awhile."

"Let me out now! You can go with me. We'll look for evidence together. You owe it to Big Bill."

"Sorry, Raider. I got to wait for the judge."

Johnson went into the front office.

Raider grabbed the plate of fried chicken. Suddenly he didn't feel so hungry. But he made himself eat. He had to keep up his strength. Even if Johnson didn't let him out, he figured the Cheyenne jailhouse couldn't hold him forever.

Becky came on Saturday.

Johnson searched the basket she brought for Raider.

The poor girl seemed frantic as she slid the food between the bars. "Raider, there's a couple of hands been shootin' their mouths off."

The big man shrugged. "Let 'em."

"No, they're sayin' that they're gonna hang you if the law don't. They say they're tired of waitin' for the judge."

He gestured toward the marshal's front office. "Don't worry, I got the law to protect me. Thanks for the bread."

She kissed him between the bars and left in a hurry.

She was back in a couple of hours, fretting worse than ever. "Marshal, they're gatherin' over at the saloon. Sayin' they're gonna come for Raider."

Johnson just shook his head. "They ain't comin' for nobody, Becky. Not as long as I'm here."

She looked back at Raider, whose face was pressed against the bars. "Honey, I'm afraid."

Johnson directed her toward the door. "Now you go on back to the Double-W, girly. There's nothin' to be afraid of."

"Hey!" Raider called, "you don't have to be rough with her."

Johnson apologized to Becky.

She left but then came back in a half hour, screaming at the lawman. "Marshal, they're comin'! All of them!"

Johnson started to console her, but then he heard it too.

Raider was hanging on to the bars. "Where's your deputies, Marshal?"

Johnson looked back at the big Pinkerton. "I ain't got but one permanent deputy, and he ain't here."

The noise was growing louder in the street.

"Let me out of here," Raider said.

"I can't."

Becky ran to the window. "They've got torches."

Johnson reached for a scattergun that leaned against the wall behind his desk. "I'm gonna put a stop to this right now."

"Let me out of here, Johnson! I want to be able to at least go out fightin'. I didn't do nothin' to deserve this."

Johnson didn't seem too worried. "This ain't nothin'."

But Raider knew a lynch mob when he heard one.

Johnson went out to meet the angry mob. They had torches and a rope tied with thirteen loops. The marshal figured they were just drunk. He immediately fired one barrel of the scattergun into the air.

"Now y'all get back to the saloon or the next barrel goes into the crowd!"

"We want the Pinkerton!"

"He shot Big Bill!"

Johnson started to tell them that he thought Raider was innocent.

Somebody launched a whiskey bottle from the back of the mob.

The bottle crashed against the marshal's skull.

Johnson grabbed his head and went down.

The lynch mob crushed over him, trying to get into the jail.

It didn't take them long to break through to the cell room.

When Raider heard them coming, he knew something had gone wrong.

"Becky, get under the desk. Hide quick!"

The girl obeyed him without hesitation.

Raider recognized some of the faces from the ranch. They opened the cell and came after him. He tried to fight. The first two went down under his fists. But most of them had guns.

They tied his hands behind his back and bore him aloft, carrying him out of the jailhouse, through the streets of Cheyenne, looking for a place to hang him.

There was a high tree at the edge of town. Raider saw the thick branches in the torchlight. Somebody threw a rope over a lower branch.

"That high enough?"

"Looks it to me!"

"Get the horse up here!"

Raider felt himself being lifted into the saddle.

The horse was led under the tree.

The noose fell over his head, tightened around his throat.

At least they put the knot on the side of his head. He'd die quicker. A snap of the neck. Dangling like a sorrowful fool.

"You got any last words, Pinkerton?"

He took a deep breath. "What y'all are doin' is wrong. You're gonna know it someday, and it's gonna haunt you the rest of your life."

He wanted them to think about it.

But they didn't get a chance.

Raider saw a man coming toward him from the edge of the crowd.

He couldn't see the man's face, but he wore a black derby.

Nobody else seemed to notice him.

They were all waiting for Raider to swing.

The man opened his coat and took out a sawed-off four-barrel scattergun.

Was he going to shoot Raider before they got a chance to hang him?

Suddenly the man's face turned up, visible in the torchlight.

He saw the lips as the man mouthed the words: *Hello, Raider!*

Who carried a four-barrel scattergun?

The gun exploded and the rope snapped over his head.

As the horse lurched forward, the shotgun man grabbed the back of the saddle and climbed on behind Raider.

He untied the big man's hands.

Raider caught the reins of the mount, guiding it out into the darkness.

Before he could blink, there was another horse right beside him.

"Don't worry," the man said behind him. "He's with us."

"Stokes!" Raider cried.

"Wagner sent us when he found out you was arrested!"

Raider wanted to inquire as to the identity of the other man, but he figured to wait until they had stopped.

"You think this is a good place to stop, Raider?"

The big man gazed up at the walls of the ravine. They had been in the saddle all night. Stokes had brought the extra mount, had had it hidden a few miles out of town. Raider had never been more glad to see anyone in his whole life.

"I wanted to come back to this ravine," he said. "Just to have a look. This is where Big Bill was shot."

His eyes fell on the blond-haired kid who was riding with Stokes.

"I'm Anderson," the kid said. "My first name is—"

"I don't wanna know your first name," Raider replied.

Stokes grimaced. "Aw, Raider, don't be like that."

"What's Wagner doin' sendin' a kid?"

"He's gotta go on his first case sometime, Raider. And he was right there beside us. Wasn't he?"

Raider emptied his lungs. "Shit. I'm sorry, Anderson."

The kid smiled. "You're really as mean as they say."

"Meaner," Stokes rejoined.

Raider couldn't fight back the smile. "Damn you, Stokes, you always pull my ass out of the fire."

"Somebody has to."

Anderson figured he had to interject a professional comment. Staring blankly toward the trail, he wondered aloud if the marshal would be coming after them. Would he know where to look for them?

Raider nodded. "You're thinkin', kid. I don't reckon Johnson is gonna worry about me. He got beaned pretty good by that mob. Even if he's still alive, he ain't gonna bother. He had started to think I was innocent anyway."

Stokes couldn't resist the needling. "Are you innocent?"

Raider pointed a finger. "Don't start with me, Henry."

Stokes held up his hands. "Hey, I was just askin'."

"I could no more have shot Big Bill Walters if he was drawin' down on me, Henry. I liked that old boy. He's still alive, thank the good Lord."

"You think you know who did it, Raider?"

"Yeah. And I reckon I could use your help, Henry. I don't know 'bout the kid here."

Anderson took offense at the remark. He puffed up like a banty rooster. At least the kid had guts.

"I work for Pinkerton and Wagner same as you," the kid said. "And I don't have to take no—"

Raider grabbed the front of his duster. "I don't have to take no neither, boy. Now, you ever search for anythin' in your life?"

The kid nodded, wide-eyed.

Raider let go of him. "Okay, then go up yonder in them trees and see what you can find."

"What am I looking for?"

"If you're gonna be a Pink, then you'll know when you see it."

Anderson scurried off to the woods above them.

"Is he armed?" Raider asked.

"Yeah, he can defend hisself."

"I was worried 'bout him shootin' me!"

"The old man sent him, Raider. It was that or lose him. He didn't like the office job."

Raider's face went slack. "Listen, Stokes... thanks for savin' me from that lynch mob."

"It's forgotten." Stokes lowered his eyes to the ground. "Now, big man, tell me what the hell we're looking for."

"Anythin' that might—"

They both turned toward the woods when they heard the kid scream.

"I knew it!" Raider cried.

They started up the slope.

Suddenly Anderson came rolling down toward them.

They both managed to get out of the way.

Anderson rolled all the way to the edge of the water at the bottom of the ravine.

They rushed to help him. He was alive. Only one wound.
Raider saw the arrow lodged in the kid's shoulder.
"Injuns," Stokes said.
It was a Crow arrow.
"No, only one Injun," Raider said. "Half Eagle."
Anderson groaned beneath them.
Raider gestured to the kid. "Look after him."
"Where you goin'?"
He started up the slope. "To catch a renegade."
"Big man!"
Raider turned to see the pistol twirling in the first light of morning.
He caught the pocket revolver in his huge hand.
It felt like a toy.
But it would have to be enough.

CHAPTER SIXTEEN

Streaks of yellow morning light cut through the evergreen branches, baking the mists out of the dewy, sloping forest.

Raider stepped carefully, silently, between the trees, keeping his eyes and ears alert with an intensity known by few white men. He had to be like the man he was chasing—part Indian, part animal.

The air was cold and foggy, and it seemed to stick to his skin.

Something rose up in front of him, fluttering between the trees.

Raider almost fired at the covey of birds that scared his heart into his throat. Partridges. That meant Half Eagle had heard them if he was nearby.

Raider eased behind a heavy clump of bushes.

The forest was quiet after the birds set down a few hundred feet away.

Something cracked.

It sounded like a dead branch crashing to the ground.

Silence.

Raider's breath fogged in the air.

WYOMING AMBUSH 149

Nothing to do but keep going.

He came out from behind the clump of bushes.

Moving again.

He had gone a few hundred feet when the covey of birds fluttered up in front of him.

Raider immediately dropped to the ground, clutching the pocket revolver. He would have to get close for a shot. Had Half Eagle spooked those birds?

For a long time, he lay belly-down, listening.

He heard footfalls.

Someone running to his right.

Raider raised up to see the Indian as he sailed headlong through the trees. He took aim. One shot with the pocket revolver, but it missed.

Then Half Eagle was gone.

Raider dropped down again, wriggling on his belly.

The renegade's laughter rolled through the trees.

Raider wished he had his rifle. But he didn't. Think like an Injun. Half Eagle had announced his presence. He wanted to fight.

It was like hunting. The most important thing was patience. Let the prey come to you.

He rose up, running himself.

When he came to a stop behind a thick tree trunk, a Crow arrow thudded in the bark right next to his head.

"You missed, Half Eagle!"

A low, warlike chant came from his right. Half Eagle was calling for help from his ancestors. Kind of like praying.

Raider hit the dirt and began to crawl.

Keep it up, he thought. Till I get there.

As if the Indian could read his mind, the chanting abruptly stopped.

Raider hesitated with his belly to the ground.

Movement ahead of him.

He couldn't really hear it, but he could see the swirling mists where the air had been disturbed.

Patience.

Let him come.

Raider saw the point of a high hat.

He thumbed back the hammer of the pocket revolver.

He had to be close if the shot was going to do the job.

Half Eagle was there for an instant.

Raider fired one shot.

Half Eagle lurched into the vapor and disappeared.

Raider thought he had missed.

He crawled over to the spot where Half Eagle had been standing.

Something dripped from above him.

A thick drop of red blood landed on his hand.

Raider looked up, marking the stain on the bark. Shoulder high. Maybe the pocket revolver had stung him after all.

Something thudded in the blood stain.

Another Crow arrow.

He heard Half Eagle running again. The Indian wanted him to know that he had not been stung too badly. Letting Raider know that he had guts.

Raider kept crawling, making his way through the forest on his belly like a snake.

He kept thinking that there were copperheads and rattlers in Wyoming, although it was too cold for them to be out.

Any self-respecting snake would be buried in a hole.

Maybe Half Eagle was heading back to his lair.

Raider decided to stand up.

An arrow whizzed by him, forcing him down again.

Half Eagle was good.

Raider hoped he was up to the challenge of a duel with the renegade.

Henry Stokes bent over, looking at the arrow in his associate's shoulder.

Anderson was shivering.

The arrow hung in the meat part of the shoulder, just under the collarbone. Stokes knew what he had to do. Arrows never came out the way they went in. Damned Injun barbs.

The kid's lips quivered. "It it bad?"

"I ain't gonna lie to you," Stokes said. "Your shoulder's never gonna be the same. But I don't think you're gonna die."

Anderson started coughing.

"Better get it over with, kid."

Stokes cut away the clothing that covered the wound. He

felt the back of the kid's shoulder. The arrowhead had almost gone through him. At least it would come out pretty easy.

He took out his whiskey bottle, dousing the wound.

The kid seemed scared. "Why'd you do that?"

He handed the bottle to Anderson. "Drink, kid. Go on."

Anderson gagged down a swallow.

Stokes had a snort himself.

The kid tried to look at the shank of the arrow that had lodged in his body. "Is it gonna hurt, Stokes?"

"Only like hell."

There was no easy way to do it.

Stokes gave the kid a bullet. "Here, bite on this."

Then he stuck a match and dropped it on the wound.

A blue flame spread over the skin, igniting the shank of the arrow.

Anderson stiffened, trying not to cry out.

Stokes pushed the arrow through and yanked it from the kid's body.

Anderson was shaking.

Stokes went to the water and filled his hat. He came back and cleaned the wound with the cold liquid. Then he doused both sides of the wound with more whiskey.

"Don't light it!" Anderson cried.

"Don't worry, I ain't. Just hold still while I get this bandaged."

It was bleeding some, but that was all right for a while.

Stokes looked back when he heard the faint report of the pocket revolver.

He wondered how the hell Raider was doing with the renegade.

Should have given him the four-barreled scattergun to work Half Eagle. What the hell kind of name was that? Surely somebody that could be easily handled by the big man from Arkansas.

Raider crawled onto the path.

He looked carefully for signs of the Indian.

Half Eagle had been on the path.

He was heading down again.

Raider smiled. Maybe he had hurt him enough to slow him

down. There were beads of dried blood on the trail. He was definitely heading for his hole.

Raider regained his feet, half expecting an arrow to go by his head.

Nothing.

He started to move slowly, listening for signs of Half Eagle.

Maybe the bird couldn't fly with a busted wing.

Then again, a wounded cougar was the most dangerous kind.

The fog began to thin out a little.

Raider heard the trickling of water.

The path narrowed down, disappearing into thick branches.

When Raider got close enough, he saw that the branches had been cut and arranged to disguise an entrance to another small ravine.

His heart began to pump harder when he saw the blood on the thick branches. He had found Half Eagle's hole. Now all he had to do was ferret him out.

He looked up, wondering if there was a way to get to the rim of the ravine. Maybe swoop down on the eagle's nest from above. He had to be careful. A cornered animal got a lot meaner with its back to the wall.

He heard splashing.

Then a whoop.

Half Eagle was treating his wound.

If he lost too much blood, he would die. Raider wanted to take him alive. See if he was connected to Artis Blaylock. Maybe Half Eagle had helped Dixon shoot Big Bill. Partners on Raider's frame-up.

Another whoop from inside the ravine.

Maybe he was doing Indian medicine.

Feeling safe in his hole.

Never thinking that the Pinkerton rattler was going to crawl in and get him.

Raider remained still, trying to figure out how he was going to do it.

Henry Stokes looked down at the kid, who was sleeping.

Anderson would be all right for a while.

Henry looked back at the trees. He knew Raider liked to work alone. Didn't tolerate any partners since Doc Weatherbee quit the agency to go get married. He knew Raider would hate it if he came to help him with the renegade.

He looked at the kid again.

Anderson would survive if he left him alone for a while.

Henry gathered himself and then started up into the trees.

Raider stayed low, squirming through the entrance to the ravine. It was a tight squeeze, but he made it. His black eyes saw the waterfall that trickled down into the middle of a crystal-clear pool of water. Steam rose off the surface of the pool. Half Eagle had found himself a hot spring.

Something bobbed up in the pool.

A head.

The Indian blew air through his nose.

He felt his shoulder and made a guttural sound.

Raider figured it was as good a time as any to make his move.

He stood up and pointed the pocket revolver at Half Eagle. "I don't want to kill you."

Half Eagle ducked below the surface of the water, fleeing like a snapping turtle.

Raider figured he could wait until he came up again.

Sure enough, the renegade surfaced and gulped for air.

"Come on out of that water," Raider told him. "Or I'll put one between your eyes."

Half Eagle touched the wound on his shoulder and cried out.

Raider gestured with the barrel of the pocket revolver. "That was for Anderson, the kid you shot with the arrow. Now come on out of there or I'll have to shoot you again."

"You ain't shootin' nobody, Pinkerton!"

The voice had come from a cavern behind the waterfall.

A rifle barrel eased out of the shadows.

"Drop the pistol, Pinkerton."

Raider strained to see the man behind the rifle.

Harley Dixon stepped into the light from above. "I said drop it."

Raider threw the pocket revolver into the hot spring.

Half Eagle dived for the pistol and came up howling, his eerie voice echoing in the hollows of the mountain.

CHAPTER SEVENTEEN

Raider lifted his hands to the sky, glaring at Harley Dixon. "So *both* of you were in on it. How'd you buy the Injun? Did Blaylock and his friends give you the money, Half Eagle?"

Dixon stepped a little closer, keeping a wary eye on the big man. "You're good, Pinkerton. But not as good as me."

Half Eagle lifted himself out of the hot spring. He stood next to Dixon. Raider got a good look at him for the first time. He was older than Raider had figured. Lined face. Dark eyes. Nose like the beak on a bird of prey.

"How'd they buy you, Half Eagle? They promise to give you your own land? Or money and firewater?"

"Nobody bought him," Dixon went on. "He found us here and he offered to work for us. Didn't want to go back to the reservation with his old man. Did you, Half Eagle?"

The Indian was looking at the bullet wound in his shoulder. He gestured to Dixon, asking him to cut out the slug. Dixon looked back at Raider.

"You're gonna fix his shoulder, Pinkerton."

Raider started to tell Dixon to kiss his ass. But then he realized that treating the wound would buy him more time.

Give him a chance to surprise Dixon. Draw out more about the scheme that had been cooked up by Artis Blaylock.

"I'm gonna need a sharp knife and a fire," Raider offered.

Dixon nodded. "Make it quick."

"You want me to kill him?" Raider said. "Somethin' like this takes a smooth hand. I might be a while."

Dixon squeezed the rifle and fired off a round at Raider's feet.

Smoke rose up and the echo rolled for a long time.

"You're gonna fix his shoulder in a hurry!" Dixon said.

Raider wasn't in any position to argue.

Raider heated the knife until the tip glowed red.

Half Eagle stared at the hot blade with a sense of fascination.

"You want somethin' to bite on?" Raider asked.

The Indian just gestured to his shoulder.

Raider lowered the knife blade to the wound.

Half Eagle flinched, but he didn't cry out. Raider started to dig. Smoke rose from the wound. Raider drew back the blade.

"Do it!" Dixon cried.

His voice filtered back through the cavern.

It was a hell of a hideout. A man could hole up forever and nobody would ever find him. Dixon had been lying low after his dirty work.

"How was it?" Raider asked. "When did Blaylock decide you'd have to kill Walters?"

"You think you know so much."

Raider shrugged. "I saw Blaylock in Denver. He said you were a fool. Said he bought you for fifty dollars."

Dixon's hateful eyes grew wide. "It was two hundred dollars!"

Raider thought about trying it then. He had the knife in his hand. Just charge, run the blade between Dixon's ribs. Dixon would probably get off a shot with the rifle. Raider might get hit.

Half Eagle made a guttural sound. He pointed to his shoulder again. Dixon waved the rifle and told Raider to get on with it.

The big man knew he could kill Half Eagle, but what good would it do?

Take the Indian with him.

First he'd hurt him a little.

He dug the point of the knife into the wound, gouging for the bullet.

Half Eagle began to squirm.

Dixon grimaced. "You're hurtin' him!"

Raider drew back the blade. "What the hell am I s'posed to do? You want the bullet out of there, don't you?"

Half Eagle made a motion to his shoulder again.

Raider knew the slug was just under the skin now. He felt it with the tip of the knife. As he twisted the point in the wound, the bullet popped out and fell to the floor of the cavern.

He hadn't intended for it come out at all.

Dixon aimed the rifle at his head. "Good-bye, Pinkerton."

"No!" Raider cried. "I got to seal the wound!"

Half Eagle grunted and nodded his head.

Dixon lowered the rifle. "All right. Go on and do it."

Raider knew he was running out of options. He stared at the fire. If he could kick some of the coals into Dixon's face. Dive at him. Take him down. Get the rifle away. Turn the table.

It would be great if he could take them alive. Witnesses to prove he was right about Blaylock. Watch the weasel-eyed conspirator swing from a rope.

"Get on with it, Pinkerton!"

Raider reached for a stick of firewood, one that glowed red on the tip. He stuck the ember to wound, searing the flesh. Half Eagle began to thrash around on the floor of the cavern.

Dixon lifted the rifle again. "That's it."

Raider threw the stick of firewood.

Dixon flinched and took aim.

He had to kick the coals.

Lunging toward the fire.

A loud explosion erupted inside the ravine.

Dixon buckled and fell forward, dropping the rifle.

Smoke filled the steamy air.

Henry Stokes moved through the mist, coming straight toward Raider. He had given Dixon all four barrels from his crazy scattergun. He stood over the body, looking down.

Raider got up and stood beside him. "Did you have to kill him, Henry?"

Stokes gawked at him. "I saved your ass!"

"I mighta got out of it. How the hell did you find me?"

Stokes stiffened with pride. "You ain't the only one who can track. Besides, I heard a rifle shot. I thought you was a goner."

Raider exhaled, his breath fogging. "No. Damn, I wish you hadn't killed him, Henry. He could have told the truth about Blaylock."

"And what is the truth?"

"Well," the big man replied, "looks like Blaylock hired Dixon to shoot Big Bill. Walters is leadin' the campaign for statehood. Blaylock wanted to get rid of Big Bill, so he hired that one. The renegade was workin' for 'em too. He . . ."

Raider gestured toward Half Eagle, but the Indian was no longer there.

"Damn!"

They both turned toward the hidden entrance to the ravine. Fog swirled around the opening.

They looked at each other.

"The kid," Stokes said.

"Leave Dixon here. We can come back for the body later."

Raider picked up the outlaw's rifle.

They had to hurry if they were going to save Anderson from the renegade.

But Half Eagle wouldn't let them leave.

As soon as they pushed through the evergreen branches, an arrow lodged in the boughs above them.

They hit the dirt.

Stokes tried to look up.

Another arrow thudded in the ground in front him, forcing his head down.

Raider shook his head. "I *had* to fix his shoulder."

"He didn't even have a shirt on," Stokes said. "He won't last long in this weather."

"Won't faze him," the big man replied. "He'll rub his body with clay and leaves. He'll treat that wound with bushes that he chews into a paste."

Stokes appreciated Raider's knowledge of Indians. "I forget that you ain't always as dumb as you seem, big 'un."

"Why are you insultin' me, Stokes?"

The man laughed. "Hell, I know it makes you mean. And right now I want you as mean as you can get."

"Reload that scattergun and hand it to me."

Stokes gave him the weapon.

Raider hefted the hand cannon. "You're a damned fool, Henry. This is the strangest firearm I ever saw."

Stokes peeked over the brush. "He's probably too far away."

"Yeah, but I can scare him."

Raider took a deep breath and stood up. "Hey, Injun dick!"

The arrow flew straight at him.

Raider caught the point in the butt of the scattergun.

Then he turned and fired in the direction of the arrow's flight, unleashing all four barrels into the forest.

As the smoke welled up, Raider heard Half Eagle moving.

"Hot damn!" Stokes cried. "You got him on the run, Raider."

They started up the trail, trying to catch the Indian.

Every few minutes, an arrow would fly past them. But Half Eagle was getting weak. His aim wasn't as good as it had been.

Raider returned fire with the scattergun, keeping him on the run.

Stokes stayed right with him, complaining that Raider had lost his pocket revolver to the Indian.

Raider just ignored the squatty Pinkerton in the dirty duster. "Damn, how long is he gonna keep runnin'?"

"You *had* to fix his shoulder," Stokes rejoined.

Raider decided to be the hunter again. "Let's go check on the kid."

"But Half Eagle—"

"Let him think he's won. Maybe he'll get cocky."

Stokes reluctantly agreed to come along. "I hate to let him get away."

"Maybe he'll turn up later. And we know where his hole is. We can always go back and wait for him."

Stokes glanced upward, into the higher slopes. "He's probably got hidin' places all over this wilderness."

"Yeah," Raider said, "and I'm sure he can hide forever. Come on, let's go check on the kid. Half Eagle can wait."

Raider started down, hoping like hell that Half Eagle would follow him.

The kid was still sleeping when they reached him.

Raider gazed carefully at the wound. Stokes had cleaned it perfectly. And there didn't seem to be any festering, the kind that came when the arrow was tipped with poison.

"Good job, Henry. He ain't got much of a fever. I b'lieve he's—"

The arrow thudded in the ground beside them.

Raider wheeled quickly and fired two barrels of the scattergun.

The noise woke the kid. He sat up and started screaming. Stokes had to settle him down.

Raider peered into the shadowed mists above them.

"You see him?" Stokes asked.

"No but—" Stokes started to say something, but Raider lifted his hand. He was listening to something. A slight echo in the fog.

Stokes stood up. "What is it?"

"Voices."

Raider watched the same path that they had taken into the ravine.

Shapes swirled in the fog.

He counted four of them.

Two had torches.

"Shit!"

It was Marshal Bick Johnson and three deputies, coming straight toward them in the hellish vapor.

CHAPTER EIGHTEEN

Stokes stood next to Raider, glaring at the lawmen. "Well, are we gonna fight 'em?"

Raider realized the marshal hadn't seen them yet. "I ain't sure. He musta heard the shotgun blasts."

Marshal Johnson paused on the trail, peering through the mist. "Who's there?"

"Fight or flee?" Stokes said.

"Stand pat. Johnson! It's me, Raider! Don't shoot!"

The marshal raised his hand when the rifle levers chortled in the hands of his deputies. "Hold your fire, men!"

Raider nodded. "That's a good sign."

Johnson moved down with his deputies in his tracks.

He stared at the fallen man when he spotted him on the ground. "What happened to him?"

"Half Eagle," Raider said. "He's up there."

Johnson nodded. "That's who we came to hunt for."

Raider eyed the lawman. "Am I still in trouble?"

"No," the marshal replied. "Big Bill can talk now. He told me that you didn't shoot him."

Raider smiled for a second. "He's talkin'!"

WYOMING AMBUSH 161

"Looks like he's gonna make it," one of the deputies offered.

Johnson sighed. "Well, I was just glad to bring you the good news. I sure didn't expect to find you here."

Stokes regarded the lawman. "So you come lookin' for Half Eagle?"

"I figgered he was the one who shot Big Bill."

Raider looked up at the trees. "It was him and Dixon."

"Dixon?" the marshal said, grimacing.

"He's dead," Raider went on. "Before he died, he confessed to me that Blaylock had hired him and Half Eagle to kill Big Bill. The old gent made it easier for 'em by comin' up here. Half Eagle's got a nest on the other side of that rise. I can take you there if you want."

Johnson waved him off. "You can rest now, Pinkerton. My men and I'll smoke him out."

Stokes laughed aloud.

Johnson glared at the man in the derby. "Somethin' funny?"

Raider gestured to the pudgy agent. "This is Henry Stokes. And that one on the ground is named Anderson. They're Pinks, just like me. Got me out of that mess at your jailhouse."

Johnson seemed embarrassed at the mention of the necktie party in Cheyenne. He knew he had handled it wrong. If the Pinks hadn't rescued Raider, he'd be six feet under by now.

"Yeah," Stokes said, "we picked up the trail just in time. Otherwise this big 'un woulda been wrongly hanged."

Johnson nodded sorrowfully. "I owe you, Raider. That's why I'm gonna have my men find Half Eagle."

"We'll help," Raider offered. "See, he's got to be taken alive. So he can point the finger at Blaylock."

Johnson assured Raider that his three deputies could take him alive.

Stokes harumped his skepticism. "You're gonna need all of us, Marshal."

"These three are the best trackers in Cheyenne. They'll have Half Eagle before nightfall."

Stokes folded his arms. "Sure they will," he said sarcastically.

Raider glared at his associate. "Henry, don't get smart-mouthed."

"We don't need any help," Johnson insisted.

"Half Eagle is good," Raider offered. "He's wounded, too. I put one in his shoulder."

Johnson was rubbing his chin. "Then he's weak?"

"Yeah, but he ain't helpless," Stokes rejoined. "He ran us around the woods flingin' arrows at us."

One of the deputies bristled. "Yeah, well he ain't gonna run *us* around. Marshal?"

Johnson pointed toward the woods. "Go get him."

Stokes shook his head. "Foolish. Purely foolish."

Raider told him to wait a while.

Sure enough, it wasn't long before the deputies came back. Two of them were carrying a wounded companion. He had taken a Crow arrow in the arm.

Stokes rested his hand on his hips. "Well, I reckon you'll want me to cut that arrow out of him."

The deputies put their fallen partner next to Anderson.

"Half Eagle came out of nowhere, Marshal!"

"It was like he wanted us to find him."

"He does," Raider said. "He figures to die fightin'. Only I don't want him dead. Stokes, fix that man's arm."

"Raider..."

He winked at the man in the derby. "Stokes, we got to cooperate with the local lawmen. You know how the old man always says that."

Stokes took out his knife. "Well, it don't look too bad."

The man screamed until the arrow was out of him.

Marshall Johnson grimaced. "I reckon that's the only way to do it."

Raider was peering up into the trees. "He's hurt, Bick. Half Eagle ain't goin' nowhere. If we don't get to him soon, he's gonna die, and then I won't have anyone to testify against Blaylock. You got to let us help."

Johnson looked at his deputies.

Both men nodded. They knew they couldn't catch Half Eagle alone. Not even in the renegade's weakened state.

Johnson turned back to Raider. "All right. What do you want to do?"

"I'm gonna need some rope," the big man replied. "Then we got to go up into the trees."

"There's rope on our horses," Stokes said. "How about you law boys? Did you bring rope?"

Johnson sent one of his men back to the horses to get more rope.

Then he glared at Stokes and Raider. "This better work, boys."

"Hell, Bick," Raider said, grinning. "It can't be any worse'n your men did."

Stokes had a devious smile on his lips. "No, can't be no worse."

Johnson turned away from the grinning Pinkerton agents. He knew they were jumping at the chance to show up the local lawmen. But the marshal didn't care, not as long as they caught Half Eagle.

Raider and Stokes moved silently through the trees, setting their snares. The mists still had not burned off, even though it was well past noon. Clouds had rolled in from the north, threatening rain or snow. They had to work quickly if they were going to get Half Eagle before nightfall.

Stokes tied a rope that hung between the trees. "Just like flushin' a Georgia white-tail."

"You got your scattergun?"

Stokes nodded.

Raider had a Winchester that had been given to him by the marshal. "I reckon we done about all we can."

"You think the law boys are ready?"

The big man from Arkansas pointed the barrel of the rifle in the air. "There's only one way to find out."

He fired a single shot.

The noise rose up through the trees.

Johnson and his men began to beat the bushes, whooping and shooting their pistols. Raider hoped they would drive Half Eagle straight into their trap. He and Stokes were standing between the Indian and his hiding place. Half Eagle would either run to them or get lost in the mountains forever.

Stokes snuck a swallow from his whiskey bottle and put it back inside the grimy duster. "I hope this works, big man."

Raider kept watching the mists as they swirled between the narrow trunks of the trees.

Then they heard somebody moving.

Stokes raised his scattergun.

Raider lifted the Winchester.

Shapes moved in the fog.

Stokes put his scattergun down. "Shit! It's the marshal and his men. We missed the..."

They turned toward another noise in the trees to their right.

"Royal flush!" Raider said. "Let's go get him."

They rushed through the mist, heading for the snare. Sure enough, Half Eagle dangled from one ankle, caught in a sapling trap that Raider had learned how to make when he was a boy. He raised the Winchester and told Half Eagle to drop his bow.

The renegade tried to notch an arrow, but he cried out and grabbed his wounded shoulder. He couldn't move it when he was upside down. The arm had probably come out of the socket.

But Half Eagle wasn't ready to give up. He reached for something with his good hand. Raider lifted the rifle when he saw the pocket revolver. One blast from the Winchester severed the rope. Half Eagle tumbled to the ground, landing on his bad shoulder.

Raider moved in to take the pocket revolver away from him.

Stokes put the barrel of the scattergun in his face. "I'd stay still if I was you, Injun."

Half Eagle finally had to admit defeat. His head fell back. He went limp. But Raider knew that was an old Indian trick. Playing possum. The minute you bent over to tie his hands, Half Eagle would try to poke your eyes out.

Johnson and his men stepped up beside the fallen renegade.

"You sure caught him," the marshal said resignedly.

He started to move toward Half Eagle.

Raider stopped him. "Not yet."

Johnson frowned, but he still heeded Raider's warning.

"Do it like this," the big man said. "Stokes, put that scattergun on top of his head. Cock it too."

Henry Stokes moved into position.

The four barrels pressed against the Indian's skull.

"Now I know you can hear me, Half Eagle."

No movement from the renegade.

"If you move while we're tyin' you up, Henry's gonna pull the trigger and blow your head off."

Still no response.

Raider gestured toward the limp body. "Okay, Johnson, you move in and grab his hands. You two grab his feet."

They didn't question Raider.

When Half Eagle was pinned, Raider quickly looped a rope around his feet. He tied it off and then used the rest to bind the renegade's hands. As soon as he was finished, Half Eagle opened his eyes and growled at them. Both of the deputies shrunk back to draw their guns.

Raider lifted his hand. "It's okay. He can't hurt you now. As soon as you get him to the ravine, check the ropes again." He started down the slope.

Henry Stokes called after him. "Hey, where the hell are you goin'?"

"To visit a friend," Raider shouted. "If you girls can't handle it without me, then you ain't worth your salt."

"Leave me with all the dirty work!" Henry cried.

The deputies were laughing at him.

"Aw, shut up, you law boys!"

He turned to call to Raider again, but the big man was gone, disappearing in the cold fog of the Wyoming autumn.

CHAPTER NINETEEN

"Hello, Becky."

Raider stood in the back doorway of the cedar lodge, gazing into the kitchen.

The girl ran to him and threw her arms around his waist, digging her face into his chest. "I didn't think you was ever comin' back."

He held her close to him. "Aw, don't talk like that. You know me. I'm tough as nails."

She looked up at him with tears in her eyes. "You do look a sight. Where the devil have you been?"

"Later, honey. I want to see Big Bill. How is he?"

Becky pointed toward the main parlor. "Why don't you go ask him? He's sittin' by the fire. He's walkin' now. I just fed him a big meal."

Raider moved past her, heading for the hearth.

Big Bill was sitting in front of the fire. He was wearing a blue robe. He looked older.

Raider grinned at him. "I heard you cleared my name with the marshal."

Walters startled at first, but then broke into a smile. "Lordy, you like to made my heart stop, Raider."

"How you feelin'?"

Walters shrugged. "It still hurts, but I get around. Reckon I'm a lucky damned man. How about you? You still a wanted man?"

Raider replied that he was free on all charges.

"So it's all wrapped up?" the rancher asked.

"Not all of it," Raider replied. "But we're on the right trail."

He'd keep right on thinking that way until he saw the judge in Cheyenne.

Half Eagle had been a model prisoner, or so the marshal said. The renegade stayed quiet, ate his meals, waited patiently for the judge, just like the rest of them. The Indian didn't say a word about his alliance with Blaylock. Raider had to wonder if they were going to get it out of him.

They were all excited about the judge's arrival. The lawbook thumper was a salty old circuit rider who had seen every imaginable crime. His name was Abel Potter, and he was known for his liberal use of the gallows to punish thieves and murderers.

Potter set the trial date for the day after his arrival.

Raider met Johnson at the jailhouse to talk about the trial. There was some question as to whether or not the Indian could be judged in a white man's court. Johnson was sure the judge would try the case. He had done so with other lawless renegades.

They went over their testimony one more time.

Raider hoped the judge would believe him about Blaylock.

Johnson wasn't so sure.

Somebody knocked on the office door.

Raider's hand strayed down on his Peacemaker, which had been returned to him along with his other belongings. "See who it is."

Johnson was surprised to find Big Bill at the door. He was clad in his fur coat, and Becky stood beside him. She ran to throw her arms around Raider's neck as soon as she saw the big man.

Raider detected a hint of jealousy in the old rancher's eyes. He winked at Walters, as if to say, "She'll be yours sooner than you think." Walters forced a smile, nodding to the big man.

"What brings you to town?" the marshal asked.

Becky answered the question. "We heard the judge got here. Big Bill wants to be there when his tormentors are sentenced to hang."

"An eye for an eye," Walters said. He grimaced, grabbing his stomach. "Still hurts a little."

Raider frowned. "You okay, Big Bill?"

Becky ran back to the old gent. "You better sit down, Daddy."

Walters eased into a chair. "Well, I may be old, but I'm still feisty."

"Maybe we ought to send for the doctor," the marshal offered.

Walters shook his head. "I'm fine. Just a little tired. I reckon I oughta go to the hotel and get some rest. That ride from the ranch is gettin' longer all the time."

Becky looked at Raider. "I'm goin' with him, honey. Is that all right with you?"

He nodded. "Take care of Big Bill. He needs you."

When they were gone, the marshal shook his head appreciatively. "That girl sure took good care of him."

"Yeah."

Johnson glanced at the big Pinkerton. "Somethin' wrong?"

"No. Have you seen Stokes?"

"He should be here soon," the marshal replied. "He put that kid on the stage."

Anderson. Raider had forgotten all about him. Stokes thought it was better to send him back to Chicago until he healed. Hell, the kid belonged behind a desk anyway.

"I just want to get it all straight, Marshal. Somehow I got to make the judge believe that Blaylock hired Dixon and the renegade. If I don't, Blaylock will walk free."

Johnson couldn't feel good about the big man's chances for implicating Blaylock. Judge Potter was a harsh magistrate, but you still had to convince him of the truth. It all hinged on what Half Eagle would say at the trial.

WYOMING AMBUSH 169

• • •

People had come from miles around to gaze at the renegade as he was led to the trial in chains.

They crowded into the courtroom, which was actually the saloon.

Some of them were taken aback when the stately-looking judge arrived in his black robes. Potter had white hair and a hard glint in his eyes. Raider saw the years on his face, the hard times of dealing with lawless scum. Half Eagle didn't have a chance.

Testimony was presented against the renegade. Raider and Stokes both spoke in detail. Judge Potter grimaced when Raider tried to mention that Artis Blaylock had hired Half Eagle and Dixon to kill Big Bill.

Potter asked as to the whereabouts of Blaylock and Dixon. Raider told him that Dixon was dead and Blaylock was still in Colorado. The judge frowned. He told Raider to go on.

When all testimony had been given against Half Eagle, the judge looked directly at the renegade. "Well, what do you have to say for yourself?"

Half Eagle kept his eyes down.

"Does he have an attorney?" the judge asked.

Marshal Johnson spoke up. "He doesn't want one."

Potter glared at the Indian. "These are pretty serious charges, Half Eagle. Did you try to kill Walters?"

Half Eagle looked up and then nodded.

Potter grimaced. "Did you kill that hired hand before you shot Walters?"

The renegade nodded again.

Raider flinched at the next question.

"Who hired you?"

Half Eagle did not reply.

"The Pinkerton says you were employed by a man named Artis Blaylock. Is that true?"

Half Eagle remained silent.

Potter banged his gavel. "Well, seein' how you confess, I sentence you to hang by the neck tomorrow mornin' at nine o'clock."

Everybody rose when Potter got out of his chair.

"Wait a minute!" Raider cried. "What about Blaylock?"

Potter turned to glare at him. "I'm sorry, son. There ain't enough evidence. And this Injun here won't speak agin' him."

Before Raider could protest further, Half Eagle let out a whooping cry. He tried to lunge toward the judge. Raider caught him and swung a fist into his face. The renegade fell backward, crashing to the floor, hitting his head.

Johnson and his men lowered rifles and pistols in the renegade's face.

"Take him back to jail!" the judge cried.

They gathered up the prisoner and started out of the courtroom.

Raider peered toward the judge. "Potter!"

The old man shook his head. "I'm sorry, son. Bring me somethin' solid and I'll see what I can do."

He left Raider standing there with a disappointed expression on his face.

Big Bill stepped up and put his hand on Raider's shoulder. "You did your best, big man."

Becky was there too. "It's okay, Raider."

But the big man still wanted Blaylock, even if there didn't seem to be any way to get him.

Half Eagle stood on the gallows, the noose around his neck.

Raider and Big Bill watched from the crowd.

The judge was there too, sitting high on horseback.

Half Eagle had refused to have the hood put over his head. He wouldn't let the preacher read to him from the Good Book. He just stood there, grinning. He shook his head when he was asked if there was anything he wanted to say.

The hangman peered toward the judge.

Potter nodded, giving the okay to pull the rope that sprang the trapdoor.

Half Eagle opened his mouth. "Blaylock hired me to kill Walters!" he cried. "Blaylock's the one!"

The trapdoor gave way.

Half Eagle fell, his neck snapping instantly.

"Wait!" Raider cried. "Don't let him die!"

But it was too late when he finally got to the renegade.

Half Eagle was dead.

WYOMING AMBUSH   171

Judge Potter and the marshal were there, with Stokes right beside them.

Raider looked at the judge. "What he said! Was that enough to bring Blaylock in for trial?"

Potter shook his head. "I'm afraid not, son. I couldn't convict a man on the word of a dead renegade."

Potter climbed back on his horse and rode away.

Johnson hung his head. "Why'd he have to say it just before the door dropped out from under him?"

Stokes sighed. "He was a damned cagey Injun."

Raider looked up suddenly, focusing on a cry from the crowd.

"Hey," a man said, "did you hear that? The Injun said that Blaylock hired him to shoot Big Bill Walters."

From somebody else: "Wasn't Blaylock the man who spoke against Walters?"

The murmur spread over the crowd.

Raider searched through the spectators until he found Big Bill. "Quick, get up and say somethin' agin' Blaylock. Use the gallows."

Walters frowned. "I ain't got nothin' to—"

"Don't you see?" Raider urged. "It's our only chance to make sure Blaylock never gets a hold on these people."

"I'm not sure—"

"Do like you did at the ranch, Walters. Speak out for statehood. There's no better time than now, before they all go home!"

Walters agreed to do it.

Raider hurried to the gallows, climbing up even as Half Eagle was swinging in a circle. "Listen up, folks."

The crowd focused their attention on him.

Raider lifted his hands. "What you saw today was a hangin'. The law took care of Half Eagle. But it won't take care of the man who really started all the trouble. A man named Artis Blaylock. You remember him. He was the one who spoke against Big Bill at the statehood caucus!"

They nodded their heads, speaking to one another.

"Now Big Bill is gonna talk to you again. Tell you about Blaylock. How we got to keep that kind out of Wyomin'."

They cheered as Walters slowly stepped up on the gallows.

Raider let him have the stage.

"My friends, I have spoken to you before, and I will speak many times before this great territory is admitted into the Union...."

Raider fell in beside Stokes and the marshal.

"Damned clever," Henry said.

Johnson eyed the big Pinkerton. "You really think this is gonna keep Blaylock out of the territory?"

"It will after I start spreadin' rumors," Raider offered. "I'm gonna say that there's a warrant for his arrest up this way. That you're still lookin' for him, Bick. And if that don't do it, I'm gonna come back and find him on my own."

Johnson knew he meant it.

Raider strode away from them. He wanted to see Becky one more time before he left. She was back at the ranch. Didn't want any part of the hanging.

Raider couldn't blame her. Even if Half Eagle had gotten his just execution, it was still a horrible business. The big man from Arkansas figured he could live without it for a while.

CHAPTER TWENTY

The girl was in the kitchen when Raider knocked on the back door.

She didn't smile at him as he entered. "Is it over?"

He nodded. "They hung him. And Big Bill was talkin' to the crowd. He's gonna make sure nobody ever deals with Artis Blaylock again."

Becky turned away from him. "You came to say good-bye to me. Didn't you! I know that's why you come."

He took off his Stetson and lowered his eyes. "Becky. I coulda rode off without sayin' a word. But I couldn't, not like that."

"You don't care about me, Raider!"

"I do," he replied. "Just not the way you want me to. I ain't like other men, Becky. I can't marry you."

She wheeled to glare at him, tears streaming down her face. "Raider, I think I'm gonna have a baby."

He didn't ask her if she thought it belonged to him.

"Becky..."

"Big Bill has asked me to marry him, Raider. And I think I'm gonna say yes. He's a nice man. Nicer than you!"

How could he argue?

"Becky..."

"But you got to do one thing for me," she said. "And you can't say no. You hear me?"

He nodded, trying to smile. She was breaking his heart. He did care about her in a way she couldn't understand. But he didn't care enough to stay on and be her husband.

"Anythin', Becky. Just name it."

"Take me upstairs and do it to me one more time. Just so I'll have somethin' to remember when I'm under Bill."

"But you're gonna marry him!"

She nodded sorrowfully. "I know. But I ain't told him yet. So I'm still a free woman."

"Okay, honey. If that's what you want."

Upstairs in the loft, they were like a young bride and groom, sharing a bed for the first time.

She was so beautiful. Raider stroked her soft skin. He kissed the insides of her thighs. Put his face between her legs, something he hadn't done with her before.

Becky responded with everything he had taught her. She wouldn't let him rest. He was worn out by the time they heard the carriage rolling to a stop in front of the lodge.

"Big Bill," he told her.

She nodded. "I'll go down to meet him."

He kissed her one last time before she climbed out of bed.

"Raider, when I see you again, it'll be like this never happened."

He said that was perfectly all right with him.

"Raider! Raider come down!"

Big Bill was calling from below.

The big man got dressed and went down to see him.

"You were right, Raider," the rancher said. "Blaylock's name is mud in this territory. And I told 'em what you said about the railroad company wantin' to do away with Wyomin'. They'll never stand for it."

Raider sighed complacently. "I hope not, Big Bill."

"They even got a name for me," Walters went on. "It's

gonna be in the newspaper this month. Know what they're callin' me?"

Raider said he didn't have the slightest idea.

"The Emperor of Wyomin'!" Walters said proudly. "Ain't that a name!"

The big man replied that the moniker fit him just fine.

Walters grimaced a little. "I better sit down. Have me a snort. How about a shot of whiskey?"

"I'm feelin' a little dry," Raider replied.

"The good stuff for my friend. Let's have a celebration. Becky! Get us some dinner!"

She was already heading for the kitchen. But she spun around, putting her hands on her hips. "Bill Walters, I'll get to it as soon as I can!"

Big Bill guffawed. "Fiery little thing. Are you gonna take her away from me, Raider?"

"No, sir." He grinned. "She ain't goin' nowhere."

Becky shook her finger at Raider. "Now don't go tellin' him that I aim to marry him. I want him to ask me again before I say yes."

Walters eyes grew wide. "Did you hear that?"

Raider nodded, still grinning. "Get the whiskey, Big Bill. We both need to fire our courage up."

"You know where I keep it, Raider!"

After a few snorts, Becky called them to dinner.

Big Bill ate lightly while the girl attended him.

She really seemed to care about Walters.

Raider felt better about leaving them.

When they were finished eating, Becky told Raider to go into the main parlor so she could be alone with Big Bill.

The big man obeyed her instantly.

He was pouring himself another whiskey when Big Bill started whooping.

The rancher came into the parlor. "She said yes!"

"Now there's a surprise," Raider replied.

"I'm gonna be a husband! Maybe a daddy!"

Sooner than you think, the big man thought.

"I'm a happy man, Raider. A damned happy man."

They had more drinks in front of the fire.

Becky joined them, snuggling in next to Big Bill.

They seemed right together.

She had come a long way from the whore shack in Elk Mountain.

"I've got ever'thing I could hope for," Walters offered.

Becky told him not to brag.

"Sorry," Walters replied. "I'm just so happy I could croak!"

Becky looked at Raider. "Hey, Raider didn't get a thing out of all this."

"That's right," Big Bill rejoined. "You're empty-handed, Raider."

He told them not to worry. Sure, he hadn't got anything out of the case, except to do his job. But it didn't matter. He hadn't been looking to profit from it in the first place.

"Besides, if I wanted to count my blessin's, Big Bill, I could ask you to pour me another drink."

The rancher figured that it would be no trouble at all.

CHAPTER TWENTY-ONE

"Mr. Pinkerton! Mr. Pinkerton!"

Allan Pinkerton had his hand on the knob of the front door, about to enter the offices of the agency.

"Mr. Pinkerton!"

He glanced up Fifth Avenue to see a man running straight toward him. He didn't recognize the gangly key operator from the telegraph office. For a moment, the big Scotsman thought he might be in danger.

"Excuse me, Mr. Pinkerton," the telegraph man said. "I got a message for you. It's from Raider."

Pinkerton stiffened, the commander who was unable to deal with familiarity from underlings. "Well, then, deliver it to Wagner as you usually do. That is the proper procedure, young man!"

The clerk's face turned bright red. "But I thought . . ."

Pinkerton went in without regarding the man's reply.

Wagner looked up as his superior passed by his desk.

"Good morning, sir."

Pinkerton slammed the door to his office.

Wagner frowned, but he wasn't too upset. Pinkerton, like

178   J. D. HARDIN

any boss, had his moods. Wagner had gotten used to it by now.

When he looked up again, the key operator was standing there.

"Yes?"

The man was still blushing. "I brought a message. It's from Raider. Ever'thing turned out all right in Wyomin'. He's free now. Him and a man named Stokes are waitin' for new assignments."

Wagner squinted at the man. "It's so nice of you to read our messages for us. That way I can rest my eyes."

The slight went over the man's head. He was still angry at Pinkerton. "A lot your boss cares! I brought this over special, and he rushes past me like I got smallpox or somethin'."

Wagner held out his hand. "Let me see the message, just for my own edification."

After he had read it, he immediately dictated the replies. The clerk wrote them down in a hurried scribble. Wagner wondered if the writing was legible, but the clerk read it back perfectly when they were finished.

"By the way," Wagner told him, "keep up the good work. And here's five dollars for your trouble."

"Gosh, thanks Mr. Wagner!"

He forgot about Pinkerton's rudeness and left the office a happy man.

After an hour had passed, Pinkerton came out to see Wagner. "Any messages?"

Wagner told him that Raider and Stokes had been dispatched to new, separate assignments.

Pinkerton nodded, then said, "I shouldn't have been so gruff with that lad from the wire office."

"Forget about it," Wagner replied. "I took care of him."

Pinkerton grunted. "Well, at least Raider's in the clear. And we can all get back to work."

He retreated to his office, leaving Wagner to his duties.

Wagner wondered how Stokes and Raider had gotten along. He had already heard from the young man he had sent with Stokes. Anderson had sent a telegram from Cheyenne, saying that he resigned from the agency.

Wagner sighed. He hated to lose a man, but at least Anderson hadn't been killed. The lad would probably do better as a Chicago policeman anyway.

Raider. The thorn in Wagner's side. One of his best agents. And one of his most dangerous. Maybe he should assign Stokes to work with him all the time. Keep the big galoot out of trouble.

But in the final assessment, Wagner decided to leave well enough alone.

EPILOGUE

Two months after he left Wyoming, Raider was in Denver again, striding down the wooden sidewalk. He was in search of Artis Blaylock, and hoped to find him by starting with the railroad company. But before he could reach the offices of Colorado Rail, he saw a most unlikely man coming in his direction.

It couldn't be!

But there he was, complete with his dirty duster and the black derby.

Henry Stokes grimaced when he saw Raider. "And I thought this was gonna be a good day."

Raider shook his head. "If I didn't know better, Henry, I'd say it was rainin' tinhorns."

"The hell you say!"

It was good-natured banter, so they shook hands.

"What are you doin' in Denver, Henry?"

Stokes shrugged. "Train duty. And you?"

"Takin' a prisoner to Boulder tomorrow. In the meantime, I thought I'd look for Artis Blaylock. See if he was still in action. You remember him, don't you?"

Stokes nodded. "I sure do. The sidewinder that was behind all that trouble up in Wyomin'. Course, I never met him, but if you'll buy me a drink, I can save you a lot of trouble."

Raider said he would even listen to Stokes for a free drink.

"Blaylock's dead," Stokes said.

Raider hesitated with the shot glass halfway to his mouth. "The hell you say!"

"Nope. I read about it in the paper last month. They hung him after a big trial."

Raider knocked back the whiskey, smiling. "I reckon all his dirty doin's finally caught up to him."

Stokes lowered his head, looking into his whiskey.

Raider frowned. "What's wrong?"

"Well, seems that his trial didn't have nothin' to do with all that business he was involved in."

"No? What'd they get him for? Horse thievin'?"

Stokes shook his head. "Nope. Word has it that he killed a woman. Some whore over in—"

Raider stood up. "Lolly!"

Stokes gaped at the big man. "Hey, Raider, where you goin'?"

Raider ran for the door.

Stokes tried to follow, but he couldn't keep up with the long strides.

He lost Raider in the back alleys of the red light district. Stokes had seen men in a hurry for women, but Raider was something else. He went back to the saloon, hoping Raider would return.

Raider saw the steps that led up to Lolly's room. Had Blaylock really killed her? He climbed the stairs and knocked.

Lolly grinned when she opened the door. "Raider!"

He threw his arms around her. "Thank God! Thank God you're alive!"

She grimaced, but then she understood. "You heard about Blaylock!"

"I surely did. When I heard he was hanged for killin' a woman, I thought for sure that—"

She laughed. "I didn't know you cared. Come on in and I'll get you some supper."

As she prepared fried steak and potatoes, she told Raider about the way that Blaylock went downhill. When word got around about his dealings in Wyoming, nobody wanted to do business with him. He just sank further and further into despair.

"You should have seen him," Lolly went on. "He came to see me a couple of times toward the end. Couldn't even do it. But I didn't laugh at him. I reckon he tried another girl, and she musta laughed. Why else would he have killed her?"

She put a full plate in front of him.

He rubbed her backside. "Think maybe I can get me a little tonight? I got the money to pay for it this time."

She smiled. "That can be arranged."

But it would have to wait until after they had dinner.

Lolly lay back naked on the bed.

Outside, snow was falling hard, but her place was as warm as the wet spot between her legs.

"Come on and get in bed, Raider. I want it."

He was undressing slowly, watching her as she writhed on the mattress. "You're one fine woman, Lolly. I'm sure glad you didn't run afoul of Blaylock."

"Just get on top of me and put it inside. Look at that big thing."

Raider grinned. "I thought you might want to kiss it."

She came off the bed, grabbing his cock, putting it in her mouth.

Raider felt a shiver as it ran the length of his body. "That's nice, Lolly. Don't stop."

But finally, she was tired of waiting.

She climbed back on the bed, spreading her legs. "If you want me to kiss it again, you better put it inside me."

He slid into bed, rolling on top of her.

Lolly arched her back, trying to get him inside.

Raider played with her, giving her a taste and then pulling back.

Lolly grabbed his ass, forcing him inside.

Her head went back. "That feels so damned good."

Raider's hips began to move, thrusting downward.

"Harder," she told him. "As hard as you . . . oh . . ."

They rocked the bed for a long time, bouncing it off the wall.

Raider felt his release coming.

His prick swelled inside her.

"Pull out, Raider. Pull . . ."

He withdrew, discharging on her stomach.

Lolly held him in her hand for a long time, massaging him, hoping he would get hard again.

Raider rolled off her, looking up at the ceiling. He smiled, thinking of how the business in Wyoming was finished. Blaylock's hanging had just taken a little longer to happen. Fate had been the final judge.

"You look satisfied, Raider."

"I am, honey. I really am."

She grabbed his cock. "Let's see if I can get you hard again."

He had his doubts, but after a few minutes, they were shaking the bed, bouncing off the wall in a clamorous consummation.

A special offer for people who enjoy reading the best Westerns published today. If you enjoyed this book, subscribe now and get ...

TWO FREE

A $5.90 VALUE—NO OBLIGATION

If you enjoyed this book and would like to read more of the very best Westerns being published today, you'll want to subscribe to True Value's Western Home Subscription Service. If you enjoyed the book you just read and want more of the most exciting, adventurous, action packed Westerns, subscribe now.

Each month the editors of True Value will select the 6 very best Westerns from America's leading publishers for special readers like you. You'll be able to preview these new titles as soon as they are published, FREE for ten days with no obligation.

TWO FREE BOOKS

When you subscribe, we'll send you your first month's shipment of the newest and best 6 Westerns for you to preview. With your first shipment, two of these books will be yours as our introductory gift to you absolutely FREE, regardless of what you decide to do. If you like them, as much as we think you will, keep all six books but pay for just 4 at the low subscriber rate of just $2.45 each. If you decide to return them, keep 2 of the titles as our gift. No obligation.

Special Subscriber Savings

When you become a True Value subscriber you'll save money several ways. First, all regular monthly selections will be billed at the low subscriber price of just $2.45 each. That's

WESTERNS!

at least a savings of $3.00 each month below the publishers price. Second, there is never any shipping, handling or other hidden charges—Free home delivery. What's more there is no minimum number of books you must buy, you may return any selection for full credit and you can cancel your subscription at any time. A TRUE VALUE!

Mail the coupon below

To start your subscription and receive 2 FREE WESTERNS, fill out the coupon below and mail it today. We'll send your first shipment which includes 2 FREE BOOKS as soon as we receive it.

Mail To:
True Value Home Subscription Services, Inc.
P.O. Box 5235
120 Brighton Road
Clifton, New Jersey 07015-5235

12222

YES! I want to start receiving the very best Westerns being published today. Send me my first shipment of 6 Westerns for me to preview FREE for 10 days. If I decide to keep them, I'll pay for just 4 of the books at the low subscriber price of $2.45 each; a total of $9.80 (a $17.70 value). Then each month I'll receive the 6 newest and best Westerns to preview Free for 10 days. If I'm not satisfied I may return them within 10 days and owe nothing. Otherwise I'll be billed at the special low subscriber rate of $2.45 each; a total of $14.70 (at least a $17.70 value) and save $3.00 off the publishers price. There are never any shipping, handling or other hidden charges. I understand I am under no obligation to purchase any number of books and I can cancel my subscription at any time, no questions asked. In any case the 2 FREE books are mine to keep.

Name _____

Address _____ Apt. # _____

City _____ State _____ Zip _____

Telephone # _____

Signature _____
(if under 18 parent or guardian must sign)
Terms and prices subject to change.
Orders subject to acceptance by True Value Home Subscription Services, Inc.

The hard-hitting, gun-slinging Pride of the Pinkertons rides solo in this action-packed series.

J.D. HARDIN'S
RAIDER

Sharpshooting Pinkertons Doc and Raider are legends in their own time, taking care of outlaws that the local sheriffs can't handle. Doc has decided to settle down and now Raider takes on the nastiest vermin the Old West has to offer single-handedly...charming the ladies along the way.

THE ANDERSON VALLEY SHOOT-OUT #22	0-425-11542-9/$2.95
THE YELLOWSTONE THIEVES #24	0-425-11619-0/$2.95
THE ARKANSAS HELLRIDER #25	0-425-11650-6/$2.95
BORDER WAR #26	0-425-11694-8/$2.95
THE EAST TEXAS DECEPTION #27	0-425-11749-9/$2.95
DEADLY AVENGERS #28	0-425-11786-3/$2.95
HIGHWAY OF DEATH #29	0-425-11839-8/$2.95
THE PINKERTON KILLERS #30	0-425-11883-5/$2.95
TOMBSTONE TERRITORY #31	0-425-11920-3/$2.95
MEXICAN SHOWDOWN #32	0-425-11972-6/$2.95
THE CALIFORNIA KID #33	0-425-12011-2/$2.95
BORDER LAW #34	0-425-12055-4/$2.95
HANGMAN'S LAW #35	0-425-12097-X/$2.95
FAST DEATH #36	0-425-12138-0/$2.95
DESERT DEATH TRAP #37	0-425-12175-5/$2.95
WYOMING AMBUSH #38	0-425-12222-0/$2.95
KILLER'S MOON #39 (Sept. '90)	0-425-12271-9/$2.95

Check book(s). Fill out coupon. Send to:

BERKLEY PUBLISHING GROUP
390 Murray Hill Pkwy., Dept. B
East Rutherford, NJ 07073

NAME_____

ADDRESS_____

CITY_____

STATE_____ZIP_____

PLEASE ALLOW 6 WEEKS FOR DELIVERY. PRICES ARE SUBJECT TO CHANGE WITHOUT NOTICE.

POSTAGE AND HANDLING:
$1.00 for one book, 25¢ for each additional. Do not exceed $3.50.

BOOK TOTAL	$____
POSTAGE & HANDLING	$____
APPLICABLE SALES TAX (CA, NJ, NY, PA)	$____
TOTAL AMOUNT DUE	$____

PAYABLE IN US FUNDS.
(No cash orders accepted.)